510

NEB

ZEN & XANDER UNDONE

ZEN & XANDER UNDONE

By AMY KATHLEEN RYAN

Houghton Mifflin
Houghton Mifflin Harcourt
Boston ✳ New York ✳ 2010

Houghton Mifflin is an imprint of
Houghton Mifflin Harcourt Publishing Company.

www.hmhbooks.com

The text of this book is set in Garamond.

Library of Congress Cataloging-in-Publication Data

Ryan, Amy Kathleen.
Zen and Xander undone / by Amy Kathleen Ryan.
p. cm.
Summary: Two teenaged sisters try to come to terms with the death of
their mother in very different ways.

ISBN 978-0-547-06248-8

[1. Sisters—Fiction. 2. Grief—Fiction. 3. Death—Fiction.
4. Family problems—Fiction.
5. Interpersonal relations—Fiction.] I. Title.

PZ7.R9476Ze 2010
[Fic]—dc22   2009049702

Manufactured in the United States of America

DOC 10 9 8 7 6 5 4 3 2 1

4500219545

FOR MY BROTHER, MICHAEL

The First Letter

My sister, Xander, causes a scandal practically everywhere she goes. Even funeral receptions, I now know.

I'm the quiet one. I spent the whole time wandering around our house, kind of dazed, an overwarm glass of lemonade clenched in my hand. Never much at ease around a bunch of people, I tried to go unseen, unnoticed, as I watched the guests serve themselves cake, or more wine, whispering together over some anecdote about Mom. As if they really knew her.

I had to admit, Grandma knew how to throw a proper funeral. She had hung huge family portraits around our living room, pictures of Xander and me with Mom and Dad at the beach, on Thanksgiving, and at the dinner we threw celebrating Dad's tenure. That was my favorite, because it captured Mom laughing, her blond head thrown back, her mouth wide, eyes screwed shut, cheeks red.

Over the archway between the living room and dining room Grandma had hung a huge banner that said, in big, scrolled letters, BON VOYAGE, MARIE. She'd chosen quivering violin music to play over the stereo, and she'd gotten the best caterer in town to serve dim sum, cold sesame noodles, stir-fried vegetables, and some kind of chicken kebab with a mysterious sauce that seemed to separate the moment it hit your plate.

People kept coming at me, hugging me, rubbing my back. I wanted to scream.

Xander never had much problem letting loose. She and Adam were both drunk from the bottle of wine they'd stolen. They were sitting on the floor in the sunroom, Adam's tie loose around his neck, Xander's fine blond hair in her eyes. She had taken off her black heels to wriggle her toes. Her dress was hiked up above her knees, and she twisted the ball of her foot into the floor, staring into space as Adam whispered in her ear.

I wove through the crowd. Aunt Doris and Nancy, Mom's best friend, were huddled over a photo album. Doris was pointing out a picture of Mom from grade school. Mom's two front teeth were missing, and apparently she used to do some trick with her tongue while Doris sang a song about a little worm coming out of its hole. "If we tried it now," Doris said, "it would be positively lewd."

It was supposed to be a joke, but it made both of them cry.

Through the screen door I watched Dad sitting on the porch steps smoking a cigarette. I'd never seen him smoking, and it was strange watching him because he was an expert at it. He sucked the blue smoke into his mouth, let it hang between his lips in a compact cloud before pulling it all the way in. His boss, the chair of the English department, was sitting with his hand on his shoulder, telling him to take some time off. "You've been wanting to write your next book for ages, James," he said through ridiculously chapped lips. "Take next year. Mason can cover the Romantics, and we'll put some grad students on your intro courses."

Dad nodded, took another mouthful of smoke, held it, held, and released.

I felt a presence behind me and turned to see Grandma standing uncomfortably close. "Well, I think this has been a success," she said. "Just the way Marie wanted it. Not too gloomy."

"Whoopee."

"You should mingle," she told me. "Some of these people drove for hours to get here."

"I don't like parties."

"You call this a party?"

"What else is it? People are drunk."

"I'm not drinking."

"No, of course not, why would you?" I spat. I didn't care about hiding my dislike for her. Not today.

"Don't be nasty, Athena," she said.

"It's Zen, Grandma. I've been Zen for years."

Her bloodshot eyes traveled to the corner where Xander and Adam were sitting. Xander had closed her eyes and was leaning her head back against the windowsill. Adam stared at her, fascination pulling his lightweight frame toward her while something else held him back. Grandma cleared her throat. "A letter came in the mail yesterday, for you and Xander. I found it in your father's bills."

"Put it with the other cards."

"No. You should see it. Go get Alexandra."

"Grandma—" I started to protest, but she held up a hand.

"Go. Get. Her." Her wrinkled lips pressed together.

I marched toward Xander, as much to get away from Grandma as to obey. "We're being summoned," I said to her.

Xander's dark eyes shifted from me to Grandma, who was standing in the middle of the room, her arms folded over her skinny frame. "What does she want?"

"She said a letter came for us."

"Ack." Xander rolled her eyes. "Tell the Droning Crone to—"

"You tell her," I said, and marched off to the kitchen to throw out the lemonade and pour myself some Coke instead.

I'd barely had a chance to rinse my glass before Grandma came barreling into the kitchen, pulling Xander by her wrist. Xander stumbled after her, her face curdled and pouty. "I don't see why it can't wait!"

Grandma went to the pile of unopened mail that sat on the ceramic tiled counter, shuffled through it, and pulled out one thin envelope. "I think you'll want to see this," she said triumphantly.

Xander glanced at it, squinted, peering at the address. "Zen," she said, her voice urgent.

I took the envelope from Grandma. It was addressed to both Xander and me in Mom's uneven, sloping handwriting.

Xander whipped it out of my hands and tore it open.

"Be careful!" I yelled, afraid she might rip whatever was inside.

Xander unfolded a single piece of Mom's light blue stationery and read it in one great gulp. I tugged the corner of the paper closer and read over her shoulder.

Dear Hellions,

I suppose I owe you an apology for dying on you before you're all the way grown up. I hate leaving a job unfinished. With that in mind, I've been writing you both lots of letters, and have arranged with someone to send these letters on special days for the next few years. The identity of this person will be kept secret because I don't want you calling up, pestering to get all your letters at once. (This means you, Xander.) There won't be much of me left on this earth for you. What there is, I want to last.

Don't feel sorry for me. And don't let anyone feel sorry for you. Pity will just make you both feel weak, and you need to be strong. Cry as much as you want, but no pity, self or other.

Even though this is the first letter you're getting from me, it's the last one I'm writing. That's because I've been trying to think of something wise to say. The problem is, now that I've had time to ponder the great beyond, I've grown to realize how overrated wisdom is. Or at least, I've become wary of people who pretend to have it. So, I guess that's my advice to you. The second someone pretends to be wise, run. But do listen to the people who care about you. They're the ones who will steer you right. Listen to each other.

Always remember how much I love you, and how much you've meant to me. Zen, you're my little chickadee, and Xander, you're my jaybird. Chase away the crows for each other, girls, and keep your nest warm.
Remember me,
Mom

As I read the last words, Xander slammed out the back door, ran to Mom's shriveled strawberry patch, and started screaming every obscenity known to humankind at the cloudy sky above. The party quieted down as people listened to her, shocked.

Grandma started to go after her, but I pushed her aside, ran down the steps and across the overgrown grass. Xander was twirling around, screaming such a streak of blue language that even I felt the need to shut her up.

"Xander, for God's sake!" I yelled at her.

She stopped twirling and faced me, a crooked grin on her lips. "That felt good."

"It didn't *sound* good," I spat.

"Come on," she said, pinching my shoulder. "Try it."

"No."

"Try a simple one to start with, then you can work your way up to the big ones. Say *ass.*"

"You're an ass, Xander."

She nodded, her pointer finger pressed against her chin as though she were a diction teacher. "I like your passion. Now try *shit.*"

"You're a shithead, Xander," I said, my voice grim.

She looked at me, but neither of us could keep a straight face, and she dissolved into a goofy grin. "You're a quick study. Twat-face."

This made me laugh.

For the next hour we traded increasingly disgusting insults complete with bodily fluids and illegal sex acts, laughing maniacally until people finally went home. Now that I think about it, the scandal that day wasn't all Xander's.

That night Xander and I slept in the same bed, Mom's pillow wedged between us. We slept like that every night until Mom's pillow stopped smelling like her and started smelling like us.

That's when the Vogel sisters went our separate ways. I threw myself into shotokan training with a kind of furious commitment, and Xander—well, she just got furious.

FRANK

YOU DEVELOP DEFENSES.

Like, whenever someone tells me how sorry they are that Mom died, I always say, "Oh, that's okay. She was a pain in the ass anyway."

This is how I sort people out now. The people who laugh are cool. The people who are shocked might turn out to be cool, or they might not. The people who get offended always turn out to be up-tight jerks.

It's true that Mom was a pain in the ass, but she was the kind of pain you get used to, like sore muscles after karate practice, or the burn when you're sinking into a hot bath. Mom was a good pain. Losing her—not so much.

Lately Xander is also a pain, but there's nothing good about it. Tonight she left the house wearing her tank top with rhinestones on the spaghetti straps, her studded belt, and her "man-getting jeans," which are ripped in all the most strategic places. If ever there was an outfit for creating trouble, she's wearing it now. And since, naturally, it's a Friday night and I don't have anything to do, I'm sitting up in Mom's old bedroom like a stupid jerk, drinking my mint tea and listening for Xander to come home. I don't know why I do this.

It's not all bad. The crickets are chirping, and my tea is warm and sweet with honey, and my legs have that nice *used* feeling they get after I do my two hundred kicks. My back is sore, but I rubbed Tiger

Balm on it and it's starting to feel better. I overdid the punching tonight, but I even like how that feels. Shotokan makes me strong.

I glance through my trigonometry textbook once more for my final on Monday. All that's left is a few papers to write and the school year is done. Then summertime. My last summer with Xander and Adam.

Through the open window, I hear a car door slam, then another. I freeze, holding my mug to my chest. Xander laughs in that mean way she does, and she says, "I didn't invite you in!"

Some guy mutters a low, angry sweet talk. I don't like the way it sounds.

She giggles again. "I think you've had enough, Hank."

"Frank," he says.

"Whatever. Good night." Silence for a second, but then I hear her voice hit a surprised register, as if she's been hit from behind.

I've pounded down the stairs and am almost to the front door when I hear her trying to reason with him. "Come on. I'm jailbait, you said so yourself. And it's past my bedtime."

"I'll let you go if you give me one more kiss."

I open the door to find Xander in the arms of a guy I've never seen before. He has a tattoo on his forearm that says "Christ is King" in scrolling letters drawn to look like a crown of thorns. He's wearing a black leather vest and ripped-up blue jeans. He doesn't see me because he's leaning in to Xander's hair to smell it, his finger snaking through a hole in her jeans. Xander is turned away from him, her face scrunched up in disgust. She sees me and rolls her eyes. "You're really pathetic, *Hank,* you know that?"

"It's *Frank.* Why are you trying to piss me off?" He's pretending to be amused, but I can tell he's angry.

"Why won't you let me go in my house?" she asks, enunciating every word like she's talking to someone who barely speaks English.

Frank finally notices me, and freezes for a second. Now that he's looking at me, I can see he's not that cute. He has a hooked nose and a goatee. His bottom lip has a sharp steel stud in it, but the piercing looks angry and red. He seems to register how young I look, and relaxes. "Don't worry, honey, she's fine," he says to me.

He laughs a little, and I can see by the porch light that his teeth are crooked, and even from where I stand his breath smells as though he hasn't brushed his teeth in recent memory. The guys Xander chooses!

Or maybe they choose her.

"I'm not moving until you let her go," I tell him.

"Well, then I guess *we'll* have to leave," he says, and pulls Xander back toward his car, murmuring in her ear as if she's an animal he needs to keep calm.

"Let me go right now!" Xander yells. She has finally stopped kidding around. I watch her prepare the move I taught her. She pulls her knee up to her chest, but she's gone too high. She misses stomping his foot by inches, and jams her ankle instead. She cries out in pain as he pulls her backwards, laughing. He thinks this is a game.

Does Xander? I can't tell.

The way he drags her fills me with a rage so hot, I can feel my brains simmering. As I've been trained, I walk across the lawn, keeping my gait steady and my eyes on my target until I'm within striking distance.

Xander sees me coming, and chides, "Oh ho, Hank, you're in for it now!"

He scoffs at her.

Xander ducks.

My roundhouse kick to his temple makes a cracking sound so loud, the crickets shut up for a second. He's stunned, and lets go of Xander, shaking his head like he has water in his ears.

"Bull's-eye!" Xander yells. She backs away from him, but stays nearby so she can get a good view.

"Who did that?" Frank tries to focus on me, but he can't believe that a skinny teenage girl just knocked his block off.

"Jesus, Hank, she must have killed one of your two brain cells," Xander says, and giggles.

A light comes on across the street—Adam's bedroom. Xander pretends not to notice, but I can see her get a little more serious.

Frank swings around and looks at me again. "What the hell was that?" He's obviously still stunned, because he's not thinking clearly. Or maybe he's just a moron.

"Frank," I say as I assume strike pose, fists raised. A sore muscle in my back screams, but I don't show my pain. "Drive away in your car, or ride away in an ambulance. Your choice."

He sways on his feet, seeming to consider my offer. His knees buckle suddenly, and he has to lean against his car.

Adam comes out of his house in his pajama bottoms, holding his aluminum baseball bat. He stares at Frank like every muscle in his body wants to bash the guy's brains in and the only thing keeping him in check is a weak hold on common sense.

Frank sees Adam and his bat, and seems to rethink the situation.

"All right, I'm leaving," Frank finally says, turning, and without looking at Xander, mutters, "Little whore."

"Oh, well, that's it, *Hank,*" she says. "You'll never get my phone number *now.*"

He mutters even nastier insults as he slowly works his way around his big rusty car and climbs in the driver's side. He sits there for a second, probably waiting for the street to stop spinning, starts his engine, and drives away.

Adam charges across the street toward us, shaking his head angrily. "Damn it, Xander."

"Oh no," Xander coos in a baby voice. "Widdle Adam is angwy."

Adam was little until about two years ago, when he shot up eight inches in ten months. Now he's almost six feet tall, but if Xander and I ever want to really get him mad, we call him Widdle Adam. Really, all we're doing is switching around his name: Adam Little. I think it's the baby talk that gets to him.

Adam has been our best friend for a decade at least, ever since he ritualistically beheaded Xander's Barbie doll and we retaliated by electrocuting his G.I. Joe with Dad's jumper cables and car battery. Adam was so intrigued by the way Joe's face melted that we tortured to death his entire platoon, until we got caught by Dad, who, when he saw the carnage, made us sit in the basement and listen to *all* of his John Lennon albums. We bonded over "Give Peace a Chance."

Adam chucks his bat onto our lawn and marches up to Xander, crossing his arms over his bare chest. "When are you going to stop?"

Even in the darkness I can see his eyes burning blue fire.

"I'm sorry, *Grandma*," she says to him, blinking, wide and innocent.

"Who was that guy?" he demands.

"Stinky Hanky."

"Franky," I say.

She sneers.

"One of these days you're going to get hurt, you know that?" Adam shakes his head. I've seen him mad at her, but tonight he's positively seething. "I'll come get you! How many times do I have to tell you that? Call me up."

"I don't want to wake your mom," she says.

"Use my cell. Jesus, Xander! It's not calculus. You don't get in a car with a guy like that."

She looks away from him, pretending she doesn't care what he says.

Adam whirls around to face me. "And you!"

"What?"

"You weigh like a hundred pounds, Zen! A black belt doesn't mean much when someone is a lot bigger than you."

"I weigh one twenty-five."

"I don't care. Don't take on these guys all by yourself. You come get me next time, do you understand?"

"The big stwong man is angwy," Xander coos. Adam turns around in time to catch her with her hands folded under her chin, batting her eyelashes.

"Xander, one of these times you'll tangle with the type of guy who won't stop."

I don't say so, but I think Frank might have been that type.

"I can take care of myself," she says. "I don't need you."

He glares at her, shaking his head, his jaw clenched. "Well, I don't need you either," he tells her, and storms off.

She wilts a little as she watches him. He picks his bat up from the yard and swings it a couple times before going back in his house. Xander blinks twice, and I almost see the beginning of tears, but she rakes her hands through her hair, and when she turns to me, she's back to the same old stubborn, dangerous Xander. "When did he become such an authoritarian?" she says before heading up the porch steps.

"You're *welcome!*" I yell after her.

"Thanks," she says, almost sincerely, before going in the house.

"Next time I won't help you," I want to tell her. But I don't. You can't tell Xander anything.

And I'll always help her, whether I want to or not.

I march after her, rehearsing a lecture under my breath, but when I follow her into the kitchen I find her sitting at the table with Dad. They're both dipping spoons into a carton of ice cream, eating slowly. Dad's blond hair is so dirty, it looks brown, and it sticks up in jagged clumps only where it isn't matted to his skull. Sabbatical has not been good for him. Without classes to teach or anywhere to be, he's sunk into a scary depression, and nothing Xander or I say helps.

"Nice to see you've emerged from the basement," I say, taking a spoon from the open drawer behind Xander and dipping it into a chocolaty swirl in the Rocky Road. "Welcome to the surface of the planet."

"Thank you," he says with mock formality. "Who was that outside?"

I open my mouth to tell him, but Xander rushes to answer. "Adam. He's lurking out there like the creep that he is."

"You two aren't getting along lately," Dad says distantly, as though he were commenting on the weather. There's no curiosity in the statement, no question. He seems much more focused on the huge mound of ice cream that he's sucking off his spoon.

"Xander had an interesting ride home tonight," I say, just to torment her.

Xander looks at me, telling me with her eyes to shut up. I shrug at her. I don't really mean to tell Dad anything. He can't handle even normal, day-to-day things, like brushing his teeth or changing into clean clothes. Basic parenting is beyond his abilities; parenting Xander would be beyond anyone's.

"As long as she's not drinking and driving," Dad says.

"Good, Dad. Your fatherly duty is dispensed with for the evening," Xander says, the smallest hint of bitterness in her voice. She pushes her chair back from the table and stands. "I'm off to bed."

She glares at me as she walks out of the room.

I consider again telling Dad about what happened, but I don't have the heart. He'd overreact, or he'd fade away. He certainly wouldn't deal with it in any kind of useful way. So instead I lean over, give him a kiss on his bearded cheek, and say, "Good night, Daddy-o."

"Good night, Athena," he says, staring into the center of a fudge swirl.

I leave the kitchen, trying not to feel that empty ache I get around Dad these days. It's not his fault, I remind myself as I round the stair banister. He lost his wife. It's nobody's fault.

That's the problem. Having no one to blame is precisely what gets me so damn mad.

MOM

"YOUR FATHER'S GOTTEN so fat lately," Mom says to me at the top of our creaky wooden stairs. "I'm almost glad I'm dead."

"That's not funny."

I talk to Mom a lot in my head, and she always answers back. I've gotten so good at listening for her, I'm almost convinced we really are talking to each other. Almost.

"Have you seen his gut lately?" she asks in the snicking sound of my feet against the floorboards as I go into the bathroom. "It has its own gravitational field."

"He's a little down."

"A *little* down? He's like one of the mole people."

"He's had a hard year. You shouldn't criticize him."

"You shouldn't kick people in the head," she tells me while I brush my teeth. "Go get your father next time."

"The guy deserved it."

"I know he did. Just for that greasy hair alone." I almost feel her slide her hand along my hair while I gargle. "And I know your father isn't much help these days."

"Xander's acting crazy and he barely notices." I click off the bathroom light and we step into the hallway. I pause to look at the window above the stairwell. If I squint, I can almost believe I see Mom's reflection standing behind me. It's probably just the double-pane glass making two of me, but I want to believe I'm seeing Mom's shoulder-length blond hair and dark eyes. Xander and I are both brown-eyed blondes, just like Mom. It's the Vogel trademark. "Xander stays out all night sometimes," I say to Mom in my head.

"She's trying to outrun her pain."

"What if she does something stupid?"

"She most certainly will. And so will you. Stupidity is part of being young."

When she says things like this, I think the voice in my mind must really be Mom. I would never say anything so annoying to myself.

I walk down the narrow hallway and go into my room. I leave the light off, and dive underneath my lilac-colored sheets. They smell funky. It's time I washed them.

I imagine her sitting on the edge of my bed, tucking her hair behind an ear. I close my eyes, and she smiles at me. "You're handling things pretty well."

"I'm trying."

"Better than your father is. He's rather boneless these days."

"I wish you were here to kick his ass."

"He's trying. It doesn't seem like it, but he is."

"Will you stay with me until I fall asleep?"

I don't hear anything more, but I feel her in the room with me. It takes me a long time to relax. I lay in the dark, remembering days when I didn't know Mom could die, and everyone was together, when the trouble Xander got in was harmless and funny.

SALT AND SUGAR

ONCE XANDER AND I sneaked into the kitchen early one morning and swapped all the salt in the house with all the sugar. Naturally, it was Xander's idea.

It wasn't the prank that was so terrible; it was the timing. We did it right before Grandma Vogel came over for her sixtieth birthday dinner.

Xander's the one who nicknamed Grandma the Droning Crone, and we all call her that, even Dad sometimes.

"Grandma doesn't converse, she comments" was the tactful way Mom would put it.

When you've done something she doesn't like, Grandma makes her withering pronouncement, then scrunches her thin lips together and looks off to the side. She wears silk flowers in her hair, and she is so hung up about proper behavior that it's like she's got a copy of *Miss Manners* clenched between her butt cheeks.

But there's one thing about Grandma Vogel that isn't prim and proper: she can't control the volume of her farts. It's very awkward, because she pretends it doesn't happen. She doesn't even say excuse me. And since she has no sense of humor about it, we all have to pretend we didn't just hear her butt hit a high C.

Outside of that, she's no fun, and we don't really like her.

Xander and I thought our salt and sugar joke would ruin Grandma's special birthday dinner, and her cake. We didn't realize the trick was also being played on Mom, who slaved in the kitchen to make beef bourguignon, and candied carrots, and a huge salad with homemade vinaigrette. She also baked from scratch a double-layer Belgian chocolate torte with raspberry sauce.

We watched Mom salt the roast with sugar, and candy the carrots with salt, and add a whole cup of salt to the cake. Xander and I started to get a little nervous. We sneaked into Xander's room, and I said, "We should tell her what we did."

"No way!" Xander grabbed the back of my hair and held my head so I'd have to listen to her. (This was before I knew karate, and it's also why I learned it.) "She's already mixed everything. We can't tell her, or we'll get in huge trouble."

I punched her in the ear, but I did see her logic. So we kept quiet and waited for the birthday dinner to begin.

I watched as Grandma cut her first bite of the roast, raised it to her lipsticked lips, took it into her mouth, and chewed it. I stole a glance at Xander, who was holding her breath.

Grandma swallowed, took a sip of her wine, and said, "I must say, Marie, this beef is quite . . . scrumptious! What did you do? Is this an Asian recipe?"

Mom took a bite, chewed the beef slowly, and nodded. "You're right. This turned out pretty good!"

The meal was yummier than yummy. The sugar made the beef a little crusty and sweet, the salt made the carrots a little savory, and the crispy salad was salty-sweet and tangy.

Dad's chest practically burst out of his dress shirt, he was so proud of Mom. He kept saying, "My little gourmet," and toasting her with his wine. He could see Grandma approved of Mom for once, and that made him happy.

Mom seemed ecstatic the meal turned out so delicious. She even laughed at the story Grandma was telling about how the Church Ladies were fighting with the Church Vicars about how to divvy up the surplus from the collection. Mom tossed her head back, her bouncy hair flashing in the candlelight, and laughed loud and wide. Mom had great big teeth, and a wide mouth, and when she laughed, the whole room seemed to whirl around her.

I looked over at Xander as everyone ate, and I could tell she was just as relieved as I was. We'd even begun to relax when Mom brought out the cake.

It was beautiful. Stripes of raspberry sauce flowed like burgundy rivers through the rich chocolate frosting. Mom put six candles on top, one for every decade, and we all sang "For She's a Jolly Good Fellow," because Grandma hates the birthday song. She thinks it's hackneyed.

Grandma's face puckered into a smile. She blew out the candles (farting a little in the process) and clapped. She *actually clapped* for Mom. Then she stood up, holding her wineglass, and made a speech: "Well, Marie, this meal has meant the world to me, and I just want you to know that I think you're a very special daughter-in-law to go to all this trouble for a bitter old broad like me." (Grandma would never have said this if she wasn't drunk.)

Then Mom, her smile practically blinding everyone at the table, cut up the cake, giving the biggest piece to Grandma. Xander and I took huge bites, because by now we were sure that somehow we'd discovered a magical cooking potion, so of course the cake would be perfect too.

Oh, but it wasn't. It tasted like bitter chocolaty mud. It was revolting.

I spit mine out right into the palm of my hand. Xander gagged. Dad dribbled the cake in a brown mess onto his plate. Mom actually swallowed her mouthful, but her eyes watered like crazy and she drank an entire tumbler of milk. Grandma primly spit hers into her napkin, narrowing her eyes at Xander and me.

What started out as a rare tension-free evening between Mom and Grandma turned into a screaming match. They weren't screaming at each other, though. Oh, no. They were screaming at us.

Grandma: "Do you realize what it means to turn sixty years old? [fart] My two granddaughters who are supposed to love and respect me sabotage my party! Is there not a shred of [fart] humanity in either of you?"

Mom: "I worked so hard all day on this meal and you *watched* me! [sniff] You stood there with smiles on your faces! [dabbing at tears in eyes] All my hard work! All that time spent on that beautiful cake! I should have known something was up when you wouldn't lick the spoon!"

Dad just sat at the table, laughing as he finished the bottle of wine.

We were grounded and stuck in the backyard during the height of summer for one full month. We never sabotaged Mom's cooking again, but ever since then, she always put a little sugar on her beef bourguignon, and extra salt on her candied carrots.

And years later, whenever Mom would tell this story, she'd laugh her head off.

Xander's List

It's not even eight o'clock when Xander barges into my room with Mom's first letter to us in her hand. "I say we find this person." She plops next to me on my bed and bounces up and down. Already she's showered and dressed in her holey jeans and a baby-doll T-shirt with a picture of a baby doll on it. It's way too small, and I can clearly see even in the dim light filtering through my curtains that she isn't wearing a bra.

Mom would never let her dress like that, not even at home.

"Find *who?*" I ask as I rub my eyes.

"Whoever has Mom's letters!" She waits for this to sink in, and when my eyes meet hers she smiles slowly at me. "I can see in your placid little countenance that you want to."

"For a hussy you sure talk pretty," I say before burying my head under my pillow.

"You bet your magnificently muscular ass I do."

It's true that I kind of do want to find the person who has the letters. Waiting is practically torture. On Christmas we got a video of Mom wishing us a Merry Christmas. Since then it's been five long months of waiting. A couple months ago Xander and I searched the house top to bottom, and then we stole Dad's keys and ransacked his office at the university. There was no sign of any letters, so we're sure Dad doesn't have them. If he knows who does, he'll never tell. We asked once, and he was outraged that we'd pry into Mom's final wishes. We should leave it at that, I know, but I've started to wonder if the person forgot about the letters, or died or something. We might never get another letter again.

Xander gets up from my bed, and I hear her rooting through my desk.

"Stop that!"

"What? Afraid I'll find your porn?"

"No, I just like my privacy."

"Ooo, bubblegum!" she warbles. "Grape. My favorite."

"Leave it!"

"Where are your pens?" She practically shoves her nose in the top drawer of my desk, fishes out a stubby pencil, and licks the lead. She turns Mom's letter over and starts to write on the back of it, but I leap out of bed and snatch it away from her. "Don't write on Mom's letter, idiot!"

She grins. "Knew that'd get you out of bed."

"No one likes a manipulative bitch."

"People like me *because* I'm manipulative," she retorts.

This isn't exactly true.

"Paper," she demands of me.

To stop her from ransacking my life, I reach under my bed, pull a page from my biology notebook, and hand it to her.

"Take a shower. I can still smell Hank on your foot," she says.

"Frank," I say as I stumble across the hall into the bathroom.

"Frank stank," she yells after me.

"And he does crank," I call back.

"Then he gives his weenie a yank!" she screams at the top of her lungs.

"Hey!" Dad yells from downstairs. "Both of you! Stifle!"

"Or you'll get your rifle?" she yells back.

"And I'll throw you off the tower of Eiffel!" he snarls.

Rhyming is kind of a Vogel thing, not that we're particularly good at it.

I step into the shower and let it pummel the sleep out of me. I wait until I can feel my bones warmed up before I start rubbing the soap into my washcloth. I love how regular soap smells. I don't need any of this fancy herbal crap Xander's always bringing home. Plain white for me.

I stay in the shower a long time, hoping Xander will lose interest in her mission. But when I come back to my room, wrapped in my fluffy green robe, she lifts up the paper she's been writing on and waves it in front of my face. "I've got four strong possibilities!" she announces.

"Solving string theory, are we?" I ask her.

"I'm off cosmology," she sighs. "I'm thinking particle physics now."

"You should try at least to *seem* humble."

"Why?"

Xander is the salutatorian of the senior class, second only to Dion Jefferson. She'd probably be valedictorian if she ever cracked a book, not that her grades even matter at this point. She got a perfect math score on her SATs, and won the National Science Fair for devising a new way to diagram quantum equations. Some reporter from the *New Scientist* wrote a tiny blurb about her, and now all the big science universities, like MIT and Caltech, are taking her out to lunch, which has swelled her head to the size of a nuclear reactor. She's just toying with them because she likes the attention. I know she'll pick MIT. Caltech is too far away.

"Don't you want to see my list?" she wheedles as I slather lotion on myself.

"Read it to me."

"Okay. Number one: Martha."

"No way."

"She's Mom's best friend since high school!"

"No, she lives like ten thousand miles away." Martha moved to Hawaii four years ago. She almost didn't make it to Mom's funeral. "Remember, the video was left on the porch."

"It could have been sent by courier," she says. "It's the perfect cover."

"That's what *you* would do, not what Mom would do. Next."

Xander must agree with me, because she moves on without a quibble. "Mr. Blackstone."

"Possible, but he'd never tell us if he was the one. Attorney-client privilege or something."

"He'd tell *me*," Xander says, twisting her hair with an evil grin. Mr. Blackstone gets all blustery around Xander, so naturally she tortures him. "Anyway, we can find out without him ever knowing."

I don't want to know what she means by this. "Next."

"Aunt Doris," she says.

"She's the most likely one," I say. Even though Mom was ten years younger than Doris, they were always very close. And Doris is within easy driving distance.

I hear a screen door slamming across the street, and pull aside the curtains to see Adam and his mom, Nancy, walking to their beat-up car. Adam is wearing a suit and tie, and Nancy is in a flowing silk dress. Xander sticks her head out the window and yells at Adam, "Nice suit! Is there a fuddy-duddy convention in town?"

"He's the keynote speaker," Nancy says as she opens her car door. "I'm very proud."

"Where are you guys going?" Xander asks.

"None of your business," Adam says as he gets into the car.

"He's surprising me," Nancy says eagerly. She bites her lower lip, which makes her buckteeth look even bigger. Nancy has kind of a stretchy, comical face, and it goes with her personality. "Why don't you girls come along?"

"Thanks for the pity invitation," Xander says. "It being Mother's Day and all, I think I'll be getting drunk instead."

"Splendid!" Nancy says, clearly choosing not to take Xander seriously. "Have a gimlet for me."

"I bet Adam's taking you to Marnie's on the Lake. Aren't you, Widdle Adam?"

He glares at her, so she must have guessed right.

"Oopsie. Did I spoil the surprise?" Xander giggles demurely. "Get their niçoise salad, Nancy! It's delicious!"

Adam starts the engine and drives off before Xander can come up with anything more to say.

Xander turns around as if none of that happened, shakes her list of suspects in my face, and says, "And of course Nancy was fourth on my list. Who do you want to check out first?"

"Mom, at the cemetery."

"Ghoulish! I hate going there."

"It's Mother's Day, for god's sake!" I yell at her.

"Fine," she says, but she mopes.

Now that I've said it out loud, suddenly the whole day seems dark and bitter. Mother's Day hurts. We're silent as I search through my drawers for something to wear.

I wriggle into my black pants. Even if Xander is dressing like a stockyard hag to go to the cemetery, I'll represent the Vogel daughters with some dignity.

"Did I miss anyone on my list?" Xander asks without really meaning it. I can never think of things she doesn't already consider.

"The list is fine. Too bad we're not asking any of them." I fight my way into the only black shirt I own, which is a turtleneck. I talk to her through the dark fabric. "They'll all deny it anyway. That's how decent people behave, after all, Xander. They respect people's dying wishes."

When I emerge from my turtleneck I see Xander's already gone. A minute later I hear a car horn and look out my window. She's waiting in the hatchback for me, in the driver's seat. When she sees me looking, she blows a huge purple bubble.

I look in my desk drawer. All my gum is gone.

Bitch.

MOTHER'S DAY

It's a good day to visit Mom. A million birds are weaving their little voices through the breeze. Mom liked birds. She could imitate birdcalls for fifteen different species, and giggled like a little girl when the birds answered her back.

Lots of puffy clouds shuffle across the sky, which is the kind of bright blue that only comes on spring days before the summer haze settles on the hills. We live in Vermont, in a college town on the shores of Lake Champlain, and our summers are blistering and humid. They're still my favorite time of year, and not just because school is out.

We park and climb up the hill to the upper part of the cemetery where Mom is. Even though it's early, I'm already wishing I hadn't worn a turtleneck. I fix my eyes on the top line of the hill as we climb, watching Mom's headstone slowly appear over the summit, until finally we're standing at the foot of Mom's grave, next to the empty plot Dad depressingly got for himself.

Xander is the first to see the letters, and she falls on her knees. They're taped to Mom's headstone, each in a plastic baggie. The writing is unmistakable.

Of course she would write to us on our first Mother's Day without her.

Xander rips hers off the headstone and leans against the tree Mom's buried under. She doesn't even seem to notice the bee buzzing around her hair as she reads. I take mine and lie down on top of Mom's grave.

> *Dear Zen,*
>
> *Happy Mother's Day, sweetheart. How's my little chickadee?*
> *Well, if the doctors are right, it should be about ten months after I've expired. I hope by now you've gotten used to my being gone. You're not the type to wallow, and neither is Xander. So I'm not worried that you've gained fifty pounds, or joined a cult. But I do hope that you're finding ways to have fun.*
> *With that in mind, there is something I would like you to do for me. It's your junior year, and I want you to go to the prom. I know you don't like to do anything girly, but I really think you could miss out on something special. Branch out of your world a little. Life isn't all jumping sidekicks, after all.*
> *And because I enjoy infuriating you from the great beyond (and also because I don't trust you to go without some pressure), I've chosen your dress and your date. Your dress should be arriving this week in the mail, and your date is Adam Little. After all, you two are good friends, and you'll have fun together.*
> *Adam agreed to this months ago, so there's no point in being embarrassed about it now. (It's remarkable what you can get people to do when you're on your deathbed.)*
> *And don't try to weasel out of this. I'm watching. Have fun, sweetie.*
> *Love always,*
> *Mom*

I can't believe Mom has done this to me.

Actually, yes I can. She was always a meddler.

I hear a cry of outrage and look over to see Xander scrunching her lips together in the way she does when she's furious. "No! No way!"

"What? Is Mom making you do something too?"

"She can't make me do anything." She smashes up her letter and throws it on the ground, but the breeze pushes at it until it starts to roll, so she runs after it.

"I'll tell you mine if you tell me yours," I say to her when she sits back down, leaning against Mom's headstone.

"She told Grandma I was coming over to spend the evening with her for Mother's Day. But I won't! I won't do it!"

"Lucky," I say. "She's making me go to the prom."

Her jaw drops and she stares at me, her dark eyes brimming with glee. "Oh, that's a good one!"

"It's not funny!"

"Are you kidding? It's hysterical!" She holds her belly and rolls on the grass. She laughs so hard, she almost makes me see the humor. Almost. "Who are you supposed to go with? All the decent guys are taken already!"

I drop my head. There's no avoiding it. She's going to find out sooner or later. "Adam."

Complete silence. "Oh. My. God."

"Yep."

"How the hell did she rope him into *that,* do you think?"

"He didn't have to be *roped!*"

"Oh, trust me. He was roped."

"What's so awful about going to the prom with me?"

"Well, for one thing, he has no chance of scoring with you. Whatsoever."

"Just because I'm not a slut like you doesn't make me totally closed off."

"Then why don't you ever go out on dates?"

"Because no one asks me."

"Because you give out ice queen signals."

"I can't help it if I'm naturally reserved."

"You're naturally frigid."

"Let's just pay our respects and get out of here." I pick at the weeds growing around the ivory-colored stone and brush away the dirt collecting in the carved letters.

Marie Lillian Vogel
1965–2007
Beloved Wife and Mother

Higher still and higher
From the earth thou springest,
Like a cloud of fire
The blue deep thou wingest,
And singing still dost soar, and soaring ever singest.

The poem is by Percy Shelley. My dad chose it for her because they met in graduate school in a class on English Romantic poetry, and because Mom loved birds so much. The poem is sort of about a bird, but it could also be about a woman. I guess it's a good choice for her tombstone, though Xander doesn't think so. She wanted to have them engrave lyrics from Mom's favorite Rolling Stones song. When Xander suggested it, Dad said, "*Nothing* Mick Jagger says is going on your mother's tombstone!"

"'Ruby Tuesday' was Mom's favorite song!"

"The lyrics don't even make sense!"

"The Stones *never* make sense! That's not the point!"

I didn't want to fight about it, but the epitaph I wanted wasn't by a poet or a rock band. It was something Mom whispered to us herself on her last day alive: "Every moment with you has been wonderful."

That's the kind of thing that should be carved in stone.

BLACKSTONE LEGAL

XANDER AND I are quiet in the car on the way home. I can't tell if Xander is angry or sad. Maybe she's both, like me. She's sitting hunched, her nose two inches from the top of the steering wheel, hanging on it as though her backbone is made of soft licorice. She's chewing my grape bubblegum at about 500 rpm, and I can tell by the way her dark eyes are darting over the street that she's thinking hard.

It's not until she rolls right by Williston Road that I get any inkling we're not headed home. "Hey, where—"

"I just want to see if he's in his office," she says. Xander always skips preliminaries like explaining who *he* is, or what office she means. She just waits for me to catch up.

It doesn't take me that long. "You want to try to pry something out of Mr. Blackstone?"

She shrugs. "Maybe. Or maybe I'll distract him while you pretend to go to the bathroom and get Mom's file."

"Oh, that's a great idea. I'm going to steal from a lawyer."

"Like he'd press charges."

"He's a *lawyer*. So he *might*."

"No one's going to send a motherless orphan to jail. You'll be fine."

"I wouldn't even know where to look."

"The files are in the back, just outside the bathroom."

"How do you know that?"

"*Hello?* Eidetic memory?" She taps at her temple. Everything Xander sees, hears, smells, touches, *everything,* she remembers, completely. I hate that about her.

"You're not the only smart one, you know," I tell her angrily. "My PSAT Verbal was—"

"Seven ninety. Yes, I know. But your math was five forty. So suck it, Vogel. Suck. It."

"You just lost your partner in crime," I tell her.

"Okay. I'll drop you off and do it myself." She bats at the turning signal, pretending that she's going to take me home, but I call her bluff. She reaches Colchester Road, our last chance to get home without backtracking, and looks at me out of the corner of her eye. I am silent, waiting. She huffs and turns the signal off, heading straight downtown. "It's a two-woman job."

"Why don't you get one of your derelict *lovers* to do it for you."

"Fine. Wait in the car," she says, knowing full well I won't.

Mr. Blackstone's office is in a pathetic-looking strip mall thing. Most of the other offices there are empty. His car is parked at an odd angle in front of the building. For a lawyer, he drives a heap. It's an ancient sedan, and tendrils of rust run along the seams of the body like they're trying to find a way in. Xander parks next to his car, and we get out.

The office is dark except for a single fluorescent light toward the back. Xander leans into the door, cupping her hand over her eyes, and knocks on the glass. The parking lot is very quiet, though there are a couple boys taking turns riding a bike that's too small for them. "He doesn't want to be bothered, Xander," I tell her.

"He will when he sees who's bothering him." She wiggles her eyebrows lasciviously.

"Gross, Xander. The man's fifty at least."

"Ha!" she yells. "Here he comes!"

From the back I see Mr. Blackstone's long-legged frame. He's a very tall man, and he has such a large paunch that he seems to lean back to counterbalance it. He's got overgrown gray hair, and a scruff of whiskers on his face as though he hasn't shaved for a few days. "Vogels!" he exclaims when he sees us.

"We saw your car," Xander says. She twists a lock of her hair, and grinds her toe into the sidewalk in a way that swivels her hips. He smiles at her with a strange mixture of lust and fatherly affection. Gross.

"Come on in! I was just having a sandwich." He leads us down the hallway to his office, which is mostly bare except for an ancient-looking oak desk and an oversize padded leather chair.

"I can't resist Sammy's Sunday Special," he says apologetically as he gestures to the absolutely enormous sandwich splayed on a paper wrapper on his desk.

"Smells good!" Xander says appreciatively.

"Want a bite?" he offers. "It's their classic Italian."

She accepts the half sandwich he offers her, opens her mouth so wide she reminds me of a python swallowing a goat, and manages to take a huge bite of the sloppy sandwich in a shamelessly provocative way. Only Xander could devour an Italian sub and make it look like she's having the most sensual experience of her young life. (She's not.) Mr. Blackstone watches her attentively.

It takes physical effort not to roll my eyes.

Once Xander swallows, she says, "Actually, Chuck, we had an ulterior motive for stopping by." She gives him a seductive little grin.

"Oh yeah?" he asks, also taking a huge bite, looking none too provocative in the process.

"Zen here has to go to the bathroom," she says, raising one eyebrow at me.

"Is that okay?" I blink a couple times. "Too much root beer."

He smiles. "Heck yeah."

I walk out. I hear Xander ask him about the Patriots, and he starts spouting off about yards gained last season or something.

It's dark in the back room, and cool. There's a kitchen table and a couple metal folding chairs, and a small refrigerator. An ancient coffeemaker on the countertop is coated with a thick film of what looks like coffee scum, if there is such a thing. Lining the back walls are about ten filing cabinets, all clearly marked. I go to the corner and carefully pull open the drawer marked V–Z. It slides open easily and quietly. I finger through the files until I find the one labeled "Vogel, Marie." I tuck it under my bulky turtleneck and shove it down the front of my pants to keep it from falling.

I go into the bathroom, flush the toilet, and run the sink for a second. When I wander back into Mr. Blackstone's office, arms folded over my middle to hide the folder, Xander is shuffling through his papers.

"Wow. Who knew divorce documents could be so boring?" she says to him, holding up a thick packet. "I was hoping for seedy details, but it's all like 'party of the first part' crap."

"Divorces aren't really seedy until you get into the depositions. Then you should see what people will do to each other!"

"I believe it!" Xander shakes her head ruefully. "A lasting attraction between two people is so rare, isn't it?" She turns her darkly fringed eyes upward at him, raises one brow. "Chuck?"

He nods nervously.

I clear my throat. "We better get going, Xander. We're meeting Dad, remember?"

At the mention of our father, Mr. Blackstone's face takes on a wary professionalism. "Oh yes, well, tell Dr. Vogel I send my regards."

"Regards. Got it," Xander says as he stands to walk us out. I'm careful to walk behind him, hugging myself like I'm cold. If his eyes weren't glued to Xander, he'd totally see the edges of the folder poking through my shirt.

He unlocks the door for us, and Xander slides out, but not before resting her hand lightly on his shoulder and smiling up at him.

He turns the color of an overripe eggplant.

Xander and I jog to the hatchback and get in. "Did you get it?" she asks me as she backs out of the parking lot. I pull the folder out from under my shirt and plop it on the dashboard. Xander doesn't wait. While she's driving, she opens the folder and starts rifling through it, looking for letters.

"Damn it," she says under her breath. "There's nothing here."

"Okay. So we broke the law for nothing."

"*You* broke the law." She smirks. "All I did was flirt."

"You know, it's not nice to lead people on like that, Xander," I say, remembering the attentive way Mr. Blackstone was watching her. "It isn't fair."

"Are you *kidding?*" she squeals. "I made his day!"

"Maybe, until he sees that Mom's file is missing."

"He won't even go looking for Mom's file."

"How do you know?"

"The will was read. Everything was doled out. Case closed," she says absently. She changes lanes as she pulls a handwritten letter from the mess of papers on the dash. It's not in Mom's handwriting, so I don't even see why she cares about it. We roll to a stop at a red light, and she bends over the letter, holding it in both hands, reading and rereading it.

"Well, if he does call the cops, I'm not protecting you, Xander. Don't think I will."

"Don't worry about the cops," she says, a strange edge to her voice. "Worry about John Phillips."

"Who's John Phillips?"

"Read it yourself." She gives me a weird sideways look just before turning onto Williston Road. She doesn't have the usual playful glint in her eye. If I had to guess, I'd say she was shocked.

I don't want to humor her, but I'm curious, so I read the letter. By the time I get to the bottom of the page, my heartbeat feels weak and unsteady.

Dear Mr. Blackstone,

As you requested, I'm writing to acknowledge receipt of the package you sent at Marie's request. I loved her very much, and her death has dealt me a terrible blow. This was a gift I gave her years ago, so it will be a beautiful reminder of her.

I thank you for your sensitivity and discretion in dealing with this matter.

Most sincerely,

John Phillips

THE STATUE

"MAYBE DAD KNOWS who he is," I suggest.

Xander is lying on my bed, kicking her bare legs at the ceiling. It's late and we've just gone through Mom's entire folder for the tenth time, but we've found nothing that tells us who John Phillips is. Xander is sucking on her third fudge bar, and I'm peeling the skins off grapes and eating them. Peeling things, anything, is something I do when I'm nervous.

"If we don't know who he is, why would Dad?" she demands. The side of her face is scrunched into my pillow, and she's looking at me very seriously.

I know what she's thinking and I don't even want to go there. "Not Mom."

"Why not? I got my sluttiness from *somewhere.*"

"It's not a possibility, Xander. Just drop it."

"Well then, answer me this: why would Mom keep John Phillips a secret from us?"

"Maybe he just never came up," I say, though my stomach tumbles. It *is* strange that we've never even heard the name before, considering Mom left him something in her will. *I loved her very much,* he'd said. And there was something more that I didn't like. The word *discretion. Thank you for your sensitivity and discretion,* it had said. Why should Mr. Blackstone be discreet? Doesn't that mean he's keeping a secret? But I still think Xander is jumping to conclusions. "There's no way Mom would ever cheat on Dad."

"Okay, then you ask Dad who he is."

"No." I finger the only other paper that mentions John Phillips. It's an addendum to Mom's will that we never saw, and I'm pretty sure Dad doesn't know about it either. It's a worksheet with lots of lines on it, like the one she used to give things away to her friends. On this worksheet, though, is only one name, and next to it are the words *Boehm fig 10203*.

"What is a Boehm fig?" I ask Xander. "Like a fig tree?"

Instead of answering my question like a polite person would do, she ignores me and fires up my laptop.

It takes forever for my computer to warm up, but she finally gets to the search engine and types in the phrase from the worksheet. A whole bunch of websites about antiques pop up. I'm even more confused than before. "What the hell?"

But Xander yells, "Oh my god!" and runs out of my room.

"Wait!" I follow her down the stairs and into the living room. Xander flips on the light and stares into Mom's curio cabinet.

Mom collected bird figurines since she was ten years old. She and her grandpa used to go bird watching together, and he's the one who started the collection for her. Every year for her birthday he bought her a different kind of bird. After he died, other people started adding to her collection, so Mom ended up with a lot of bird statues. She loved them all, and she would sometimes take one out and look at it, smiling. I don't think she liked the birds so much because they were valuable or anything. I think she liked them because they reminded her of people she loved.

I get it, all in a flash. Boehm fig is a porcelain figurine. Boehm must be the company.

Xander is peering through the glass in the cabinet door, tapping her finger on her chin, thinking hard. "Which one is missing?"

For once, I'm the one to understand something before Xander does. "The lovebirds," I say simply. I know that's the missing statue because it was my favorite one. I used to look at it when I was little and imagine that the two birds were alive and flying in our living room.

"You're right. Those damn lovebirds! They're missing!" She whirls around and grabs my shoulders. "*Lovebirds,* Zen!"

"That doesn't mean anything," I say, but I sound a lot less certain than I'd like to.

"Oh, come *on.* Do I have to list the evidence for you?"

"You're crazy if you think for one second Mom would do that!" I hiss.

"Do what?" Dad has crept up from his basement bedroom, his hair matted on one side, his potbelly struggling to break through his dirty white T-shirt. I should hide all the peanut butter from him. It's practically all he eats anymore. "What are you two talking about?"

I look at Xander, waiting for her to come up with the perfect cover. She always does. "I was thinking we should look into how valuable Mom's statues are. Maybe Mom meant to sell them someday."

Dad's scraggly blond eyebrows mash downward. "We will never sell your mother's birds, Alexandra."

Xander's voice gets thready. "I don't want to either. I was just speculating . . ."

"Maybe a few of them are worth a hundred bucks. Most of them are worthless. Hardly worth having them appraised." Dad seems offended. "Now I don't want to hear talk of this again," he says quietly before turning away.

We watch Dad shuffle into the kitchen. Xander just stands there, totally ashamed. It serves her right for suggesting that Mom would have an affair.

"Thanks for coming to my rescue there, Zen," she hisses. "Now Dad thinks I'm a grave robber."

"So?" I shrug before heading back upstairs.

"Where are you going?"

"To bed."

"You don't want to know about this?"

The question makes me extremely nervous, and I shake my head. "I don't think I do." I feel like Xander and I are wandering into an area where we don't belong. I can almost feel Mom begging us not to go any further. I imagine her standing in the dark corner behind the curio cabinet, her hands clenched under her chin, mouthing the words *please don't.*

Xander tromps behind me into my room and closes the door so Dad can't hear. "Zen, we can't let it lie."

"*You* can't. I can do whatever I want."

"Are you telling me that you're fine with not knowing who John Phillips is and why Mom sent him . . ." She pauses, casting a sideways glance at my laptop. She sits down again, briefly examines the addendum to Mom's will, and types some more.

"Can't you do that in your own room?" I say as I crawl under my covers. I'm suddenly achy and tired, like I've been racked with the flu.

"Aren't you curious how much that statue is worth, Zen?"

Xander's knowing tone makes me look at her.

My marrow feels cold, and I pull my knees up to my chest. "How do you know it's the same statue?"

"Because the numbers here, ten-two-oh-three, that's a number the company uses to identify its pieces. And look—" She tips the computer monitor at me. On the screen is a perfect image of the two white birds on the apple blossom branch. There's no mistaking it. It's Mom's figurine. "It's a limited edition collectible. Only two hundred were made." She blinks at the screen, as though she can't believe what she's seeing. "It's worth six thousand dollars."

MOM AND DAD

ALL FAMILIES HAVE STORIES. After Xander leaves I lie alone in the dark and file through the Vogel Collection in my mind, searching for some hint, some little slip from Mom about John Phillips. But all I can think about is the story of how my parents met, as told by James and Marie Vogel:

"Your mother was the hottest little librarian on campus."

"There was Betty Masterson."

"Yuck! Who needs breasts that big?"

"You noticed her *breasts?*" Mock indignation.

Uncomfortable pause for comedic effect. "*Anyway.* As I was saying, your mother was the hottest little librarian on campus except for Betty Masterson."

Mom hits him with whatever is available—napkin, couch cushion, spatula, depending on which room we're in. "And your father was the subject of much speculation among the women of Dartmouth College."

"I was very mysterious."

"Despite your devotion to corduroy."

"The first thing I noticed about your mother was her tiny waist. She was looking for a reserved book for some oaf in line ahead of me when I spotted her. I thought she embodied the Platonic ideal of the librarian, in her plaid skirt and clogs."

"I never wore a clog in my life."

"Her clogs made her stumble so cutely."

"*Cutely* isn't a word. And they were penny loafers."

"She checked out my enormous array of books on Eliot—"

"It was Yeats—"

"Eliot's *Wasteland*—yes, that's right—"

"Yeats's *Sailing to Byzantium*—"

"Who is telling this story?"

"If by 'story' you mean 'pure fiction,' then you are."

"I was researching for an article on Yeats."

"Ha! See, I was right!"

"I mean Eliot, and she checked out my books. She stamped them all with her little rubber stamp—"

"These were the days before libraries gave people those awful computer receipts."

"And she piled them all very neatly for me before she lifted her eyes to my face. She smiled that dazzling smile of hers—"

"I never smiled in those days—"

"—and she said, 'Have a nice day.' I do not think she noticed me at all."

"But I did, because I remembered you and your corduroy pants when you sat down next to me in our Romantic poetry class a month later."

"Ah, and you spoke so intelligently about that poem by Wordsworth—"

"I hate Wordsworth. It was *Rime of the Ancient Mariner* by Coleridge."

"She spoke so intelligently about Wordsworth's 'By the Sea' that I realized not only was she a hot librarian, but she was a hot, *smart* librarian."

"And he begged me to go out with him."

"I *casually inquired* whether she would be interested in joining me and my colleagues for a friendly drink."

"Ten drinks, more like."

"We might have overindulged—"

"You might have vomited—"

"At any rate, somewhere between giddiness and total ruination, I worked up the courage to ask her on a real date—"

"He made me pay for my half—"

"She insisted on contributing to the bill, and that is the only time I've ever allowed her to pay for her own meal."

"Well. That much *is* true."

"We dated for over a year before I had to transfer to the Ph.D. program at Harvard. She wouldn't follow me."

"I had to finish my master's!"

"She could have applied to Harvard."

"I don't have your mind, James."

"But I waited for her."

"And I came."

At this they would smile into each other's eyes, and sometimes even kiss.

At which point Xander and I would double over, pretending to throw up.

THE DRESS AND MY BACK

EVEN FROM THE GRAVE, Mom has terrible timing. It's the next day, and I'm racing through the house, looking for my gi, or my "karate pajamas" as Xander calls them, when the doorbell rings. I hear Xander open the door, probably still wearing the jeans and T-shirt she'd worn last night. She thanks someone before slamming the door and screaming, "Zen! Package! It's from Mom!"

I hear the sound of ripping paper.

"I know it's my stupid prom dress. Is there a note from Mom in it?" I call down.

"No!" she answers.

"Then I'll look at it later!" I have only forty minutes to get to practice, and it's a twenty-minute drive. I like to get there early enough to stretch out and meditate.

"Oh, it's nice, Zen! Get down here!"

She sounds really excited, probably because I haven't worn a dress since I was twelve. People think it's because I'm some kind of tomboy, but that's not it. I happen to know that I have a nice butt and long legs, so I look better in pants. Better than I ever would wearing a stupid skirt and stockings, which always crawl down my crotch and get twisted at the ankles. I hate stockings. The only thing they're good for is to wear over your face during an armed robbery.

"Zen, I want you to try this dress on!"

"I don't have time! I can't find my gi!"

I hear her rummaging around downstairs like she's looking for it. I come down because it's very unlike Xander to help me do anything. "Have you seen my gi?" I ask her suspiciously.

She's standing in the middle of a pile of tissue paper, shuffling through the mess, mumbling, "I can't find it."

"Can't find what?"

"There's no return address here. It didn't come from a store, so probably whoever sent it is the one sending the letters." She sits on the coffee table, and it cracks a little further toward the floor. One of these days she's going to get a huge splinter in her ass from that thing. She smiles at me, raises one eyebrow, and lifts the dress up from the middle of the pile in front of her. "Oooh, look at the purdy dress! Ain't it just the most?"

It's shimmery and silky and light and airy. The color is sort of bone, sort of ivory, sort of tan. At least it isn't pink, but it doesn't matter. "I hate it."

"You do not!"

"Have you seen my gi?"

"Yes. I hid it. Try this dress on right now."

"Give me my gi this instant!" I stomp on the floor with each word.

"Hey up there!" Dad calls from the basement. Ever since I hid the peanut butter, he hardly comes upstairs anymore. "Stop stomping!"

"We're only romping!" Xander calls, a lopsided grin on her face.

"Cut it out or I'll give you a whomping!"

Xander shakes the dress at me. The little beads in the bodice sparkle madly. "Try it on and I'll give you your gi!"

I look at the clock. I have only thirty minutes to get there. I've already lost my meditation time, but I can still stretch if I hurry. "Fine. I'll try it on."

She tosses it at me, and I take it into the downstairs bathroom, rip off my T-shirt, and pull the dress on over my jeans. I launch myself out the door and into the living room without even bothering to look in the mirror.

Xander's eyebrows shoot up. "Wow. You have tits!"

"Shut up!" I yell.

"No, really, they're right there." She points with both hands. "I wouldn't have believed it if you'd told me." Xander makes a slow circle around me, looking me up and down. "It's really nice on you, Zen. Hold still while I zip." I feel her fiddling with the back of the dress, and suddenly the bodice is pulled snug. "It fits too."

I take a deep breath, hoping to prove that it's too tight, but she's right. The fit is perfect. "It's fine. Now can I have my gi?"

"Did you look at yourself in the mirror?"

"That wasn't part of the deal!"

"Come on! Just take a look. Ow!"

I've grabbed her left wrist and twisted her arm so that she's totally immobilized, and I steer her around the room. "Am I getting warmer? Warmer?"

"That hurts! Let me go!"

"Colder?" I twist her arm a little more, and I suddenly have her complete cooperation.

"Warmer!" she says when I point her toward the kitchen. I push her through the door and twirl her around, pointing first at the sink. "Colder!" she cries. I spin and point toward the cabinets. "Colder!"

"You know, you could just say where it is," I remind her.

"Oh yeah. It's in the refrigerator."

I've known her too long to release her before I've confirmed this. I walk her over to the fridge. "Open it."

With her free hand she yanks open the door, and I see my poor gi draped over two different plates of leftovers. "Where's my belt?"

"Crisper," she says. "Let me go!"

I release her wrist and get everything out. There's mayonnaise on my gi, and my belt now smells like onions. "Damn it, Xander!"

She plops down at the kitchen table, rubbing the back of her arm. "One of these days I'm going to get some steel knuckles."

"Or, you could avoid confrontations by not touching my stuff!" I throw the dress at her for emphasis.

"I just thought you should try it on. See how *pretty* it is!" She fingers the silk wistfully, and I realize she's sad. "You don't know how lucky you are."

Maybe she's right. For Mother's Day I got a pretty dress and a date to the prom. She got an order to go see Grandma, not that she obeyed. Instead she went out with her skanky friend Margot and came home drunk at three a.m. Xander's misbehavior aside, I have to agree with her that it isn't really fair. Mom probably assumed that Xander would find her own date and dress for the prom, but she's not going this year. She got asked by plenty of guys, but she turned them all down. When I asked her about it, she mysteriously said, "I didn't want to go with those guys." I'd started to think that she didn't want to go at all, but the way she's looking at my dress, I realize she really does.

"If you want it, you can have it," I tell her. I hop into my white pants and wrap the gi around my waist, tying it closed with my new black belt that I won this fall.

"I don't want it. This is your dress."

"You could come with Adam and me," I suggest, knowing full well she won't like it.

This makes her angry. She folds the dress roughly and plops it on the bench between us. "I don't need your pity."

"I don't pity you," I say. "We could all go as friends."

She shakes her head. "That's not the way I want it." She tries to muffle her anger. "Aren't you late for practice?"

I leap up from the bench. Now I don't even have stretching time. "Damn. Where are the car keys?"

"Bowl by the door."

I bolt outside and to the car. I get lucky with the traffic lights, so it takes me only fifteen minutes to drive to the dojo, which is in the second floor of an office building. It shares a space with a dance studio, so there are mirrors covering the walls, and wooden rails for people to hold while they stretch. I inhale the smell of our dojo deep into me. It's a musty smell, like old paper, but I love it anyway.

The first thing I notice is that the mats aren't set up on the floor yet, so I guess I won't be able to stretch at all. I pull them off the pile and start dragging them into place. They're superheavy, and I feel the sore muscle in my back give way. My back hasn't really felt right since the night I kicked Frank in the head. It was still totally worth it.

Mark comes out of his office. "Zen!" He bows, and I bow. My back complains. I better take a time out and stretch no matter what. "What's the good news?"

"My belt smells like onions. What's news with yous?"

"My belt smells like rancid turtle effluence." Mark's son has a turtle who throws up a lot. Turtles are very sensitive pets, apparently.

"Interesting," I say, like I really mean it. "I've never smelled that. What's it like?"

"It smells a lot like rancid gecko effluence."

"You guys should get a dog."

"Oh yeah? Dog barf smells better?"

"Oh. Much," I say, and roll my eyes. I consider telling him about how I kicked Frank in the head, but I think better of it. Mark might lecture me about the responsible use of my skills. "What's on the program today?"

"Escape from bear hug," he says with real enthusiasm. "Ready to get thrown to the floor eleven times?"

"Only eleven?"

As instructors, we have to let the kids practice the moves on us before we let them loose on one another. It's the only way to make sure things stay safe. Mark does half the class and I do the other half.

The first student comes in—Lacy Jackson, a tiny fifth-grader who wears glasses and has an evil overbite. She folds her hands and bows deeply in front of me. I bow at her, and she goes and sits down, her legs tucked primly under her the way we've taught them.

"Lacy Jackson!" Mark yells, startling her. "You win the prize for arriving first! You get to pick out our warm-up routine!"

"The swan!" she squeaks. The kids don't know that the warm-ups have all the same moves, we just mix up the order and give them different animal names.

"The swan it is!" Mark yells, and then he does a headstand to make her laugh.

Mark loves, and I mean *loves* teaching shotokan, but then again he seems to love everything he does. When I hear the words *good attitude,* I think of Mark. He's supershort, and he has a wide nose that's so turned up, it makes him look a little like an anteater. His weird nose didn't stop him from getting a great wife, though, and she's just as happy as he is. So are their two toddlers.

It's nice to be around such happy people. That's probably why I've kept coming for so long, even when Mom was sick. It really helped, getting a break from watching Mom's body fall apart. When the doctors finally told us there was nothing more they could do and I thought my world was ending, Mark hired me as his assistant. He said there really wasn't anything more he could teach me. So I got my black belt, and now I'm teaching. Sometimes when I'm here I think I'm almost as happy as Mark is. That is, when I'm not thinking of Mom.

Mark and I arrange the mats on the floor as the kids trickle in. Today we're teaching a bunch of fifth-graders, which is my favorite age because they're finally big enough to start doing some real shotokan without risk of injury.

"Hai!" Mark yells at them to start class, and he bows.

"Hai!" all the kids say as they bow back.

We go through the motions of the swan, which warms me up

nicely. I get some stretching in, too, but not as much as I like. Mark talks them through the new move, demonstrating it on a big kid named Nicolas Renfro. Nick is probably the nicest kid I've ever met. He's got sandy blond hair and tons of freckles all over his face and neck and hands. Though he's a little fat and taller than I am, he still has a little-boy voice, which makes him adorable.

Nick puts Mark in a bear hug, as instructed. I watch, twisting around a little, trying to work the kink out of my back. I finally feel it loosen just as I hear Mark say, "Ready? Let's do it, Nick!"

Mark bends and twists his body, making Nick lose his balance just the way he's supposed to. He falls down, laughing.

If Mark had really done that move with full and proper force, Nick would not be laughing. As instructors, we have to be gentle.

"Okay!" Mark claps. "Let's split into groups and learn the move!"

I go stand in front of the line of kids I'm supposed to teach. Nick is first. It seems like he's always in front when I'm leading his group. I'm starting to think he might have a little crush on me. He licks his lips nervously as I come up behind him. "Don't worry, Nick," I tell him. "Just bend down the same way Mark did until you feel me lose my balance, and then roll me over, okay?"

"Okay," he says in his cute little-boy voice. It's funny he's interested in shotokan. He wouldn't hurt a fly.

I wrap my arms around him tightly, saying to the kids behind him, "Watch carefully and learn from what Nick does." Little Lacy Jackson nods her pigtailed head.

When I feel like I have a lock on Nick, I whisper, "Okay, Nick. Go!"

He holds perfectly still.

"Nick, it's okay. Do the move."

"I don't want to hurt you." He says it so softly that I almost forget he outweighs me.

"Nick, I've been doing this a long time. I know how to fall."

"I know, but . . ."

"Trust me. You won't hurt me." I hug him as hard as I can and lift him off his feet. A nagging pain pulls at the left side of my spine. I should not have tried to lift such a big kid. But it's not so bad that I can't hide it, and I set him back down. "See how strong I am?"

"Uh-huh." He seems a little more sure.

"Imagine I'm a big bully," I tell him, remembering that guy Frank again, the guy who tried to force Xander into his car, and it makes me hate him all over again. But I have a job to do. I smile at the rest of the students, who are watching Nick and me expectantly. "Okay, on the count of three. One . . . two . . . three!"

Nick bends over and twists just the way he's supposed to.

I scream as pain tears through my back.

The next thing I know I'm staring up at the ceiling with Nick's chubby face looking down at me. "Are you okay?"

Yes.

Am I?

I thought I said yes, but maybe I didn't speak. I couldn't have spoken, actually, because I'm holding my breath.

I have a feeling it's going to hurt to breathe.

"You said I wouldn't hurt you!" Nick squeals.

Mark's face appears over me. "You okay?"

I take a tentative breath, and it hurts only a little when my rib cage expands, which is good, considering I need air to live.

I smile and try to pick myself up, if only to keep Nick from crying. I get halfway upright when my back erupts in pain. "Oh, shit," I say.

The kids gasp. No swearing in the dojo.

Slowly I ease myself upright until I'm sitting.

Mark winces for me. "Oh, Zen. Don't move."

I lie down flat again. Tears squeeze out of my eyes; my back hurts so much.

Nick lies down on the floor next to me, his chubby cheek scrunched against the mat. "I'm sorry," he whispers.

"It's okay," I whisper back.

His whole body seems to collapse in shame, and tears pop out of his eyes.

The kid who just kicked my ass starts crying like a baby.

PAIN

"Hiya, slug."

"Hi, Mom." I stare at the same crack in my ceiling that I've been staring at for two days. I imagine her hiding inside the tiny fissure in the plaster, watching me.

"How's the ol' spine feeling?"

"It hurts."

"*How* does it hurt? Is it achy?"

"No."

"Tingly? Like when your foot falls asleep?"

"No."

"Sore? Like a bruise kind of?"

"Why does it matter? It just hurts!"

"I'm just wondering. I'd rub it for you if I could."

"Thanks for the thought."

"All I can *do* is think." She's silent for a moment, pacing up and down the crack in the ceiling. Then she gets big and floats down to sit on my bed. "I know! It's throbbing. Is that it?"

"Yes!" I say just to shut her up.

"Yeah. I remember throbbing. Throbbing was not my favorite pain."

"You had a favorite pain?"

"Soreness. That's the best one."

"Whatever you say."

"I had a lot of time to contemplate the different types of pain when you were at school and I was stuck in my room all day. I ranked them. Soreness, tingling, achiness, throbbing, burning, stinging, and agony." She shudders.

"Stinging is worse than burning?"

"Yeah, I know. It's surprising. I wouldn't have taken this view before I got sick. But yes, I'd say that stinging has a deeper kind of oomph to it. It's more physical."

"I couldn't disagree more. Burning is much worse."

"Get back to me when you've had cancer."

"Whatever."

"You know why you're in pain, right?"

"I was thrown by a student."

"That's not when you hurt your back and you know it."

"I'm not going into it, Mom. The guy was trying to hurt Xander and I stopped him."

She's quiet for a minute, but I know by the quality of her silence that this isn't over. Finally I feel her nestle into the cup of my ear. "When I was alive, I hurt myself the worst when I was doing something I shouldn't be doing."

"We've already been through this."

"Zen, you know you screwed up. It scares me that you won't admit it."

I try to shut out Mom's words, but they've wormed their way into my brain, and now I doubt myself. Was I really just trying to protect Xander? Or was I looking for a head to kick? It did feel awfully good to kick that guy, even though I tore something in my back doing it. Should it feel good to hurt someone?

I hear sounds from the neighborhood through the haze of the Vicodin the doctor gave me. Slamming car doors, the hum of a lawn mower, one of our neighbors shouting at his kids. I wish I could go outside, but I'm stuck here. My eyes trail to the folder lying open on my desk, the one we stole from Mom's lawyer.

"You should just stop it," Mom says bitterly. I almost forgot she was here.

"Stop what?"

"You know what. That folder is none of your business."

"The whole thing was Xander's idea."

"I may be dead, but I still have feelings."

"I know!"

"Tell your sister I said to stop."

"Like she'd believe me."

She says nothing to this. Xander is too scientific to believe in ghosts. She'd probably recommend I see a psychiatrist if I told her I still talk to Mom.

"So who is John Phillips, Mom?" I ask her.

I feel a wistful sigh moving through the air in the room, and then she's gone.

RAILROAD

I[T]'[S SUNNY OUT], and I'm spraying all the weeds on our lawn with some supposedly organic, environmentally friendly poison. I've spent the last three days in bed, nursing a bad muscle sprain, and it feels great to be out of my bedroom. The doctor said that I'll get better faster if I can resume light activity, but no, absolutely no shotokan practice for at least three weeks.

It's killing me.

It's hot outside, and I can practically feel my shoulders crisping in the sun. I should do this later, but I don't want to go in the house because Xander is obsessing about John Phillips, and I don't want to get pulled into her psychodrama.

Spraying weeds is boring. Normally I would mix it up with a little shotokan practice. Spray. Side kick. Spray. Elbow strike. Spray. Middle block. But just standing long enough to aim and spray is already as much as my back can take. I still can't bend over, so my aim isn't so good.

"Hey! Zen!" I hear from across the street, and look up to see Adam coming over. He's wearing a straw gardener's hat, cargo shorts, and his old brown sandals, which are encrusted with mud. He must have been working out back in his mom's garden. "How's it going?"

"Okay," I say, keeping my head down as I spray another dandelion. "You all ready for finals week?"

"More or less. I only have two tests. The rest are papers." Adam is a very good student. He ranks tenth in the class, only because he got a C+ in home economics his freshman year. He isn't like Xander, though. He has to study. "You ready for your trig final?" he asks me.

"I think so." I shrug. My grades aren't the greatest these days, but I don't really care. After Mom died, little stuff no longer seems to matter. I don't even think of school when I'm not there. "I'll eke by."

"So." He casts his dark blue eyes over the roof of our house. "Did that guy ever come back?"

I know exactly who he's talking about. Every time I remember, I get angry all over again. "Haven't seen him."

"That's good." He twists his face into an uncertain smile, crosses his arms over his chest, uncrosses them, and jams his toe into a hunk of crabgrass I just sprayed. "Get any interesting mail recently?"

By the fidgety look in his eyes, I can tell he's talking about the prom.

"Adam." I take my rubber gloves off and lead him over to our porch to sit on the steps. Sitting next to him makes me wish I was lithe and sexy like Xander, but I'll have to settle for "athletic." "You really don't have to do this."

He seems a little disappointed. "But your mom said—"

"I know. It's just, the prom really isn't my style."

"Mine neither." He grabs hold of my wrist and pulls it so that I have to look at him. "I'm picking you up at six o'clock on Friday. You'll be wearing a nice dress, and I'll be in a tux. We'll have dinner at Il Maestro's, and then we're going to the prom. We'll get our pictures taken, and we'll dance to a few songs and have some terrible punch. Then we will heave huge sighs of relief as we leave. After that, we're going to get some ice cream, and then I'm bringing you home so you can practice cracking skulls, or whatever it is you do in your spare time. Okay?"

"*Why?*" is all I can say.

In that one word are lots of questions I can't ask. *Why* is Mom doing this? *Why* did she choose Adam? *Why* can't I just remember her fondly and escape all the meddling in my life like other mother-less orphans get to do?

"Your mom wanted it."

"What did she say to you?"

He pauses, seeming to gauge something about me before answering: "She told me you're too self-sufficient, and you cut yourself off from other people, and that she thought going to the prom would—"

"—get me out of my comfort zone?" I finish the thought for him. My mom was always saying this. She was probably the only mother in America who *liked* it when her kids were uncomfortable.

He doesn't answer. He just smiles.

Just then the front door slaps open, and Xander is standing on the porch wearing her thready cutoffs, holding three Popsicles. "Who wants root beer?" she asks, knowing Adam will take it.

Soon all three of us are eating our Popsicles on the porch steps just like in the old days before Xander and Adam started fighting so much.

"Remember that time we found the robin's egg?" Xander says.

Adam smiles. "Of course."

"Didn't you want to kill it, Xander?" I point out helpfully.

"I just wanted to see what was inside!"

Even back then, when they were ten and I was eight, our personalities were fully formed. Xander was the scientist. She wanted to break the little blue egg open and look at the bird fetus inside. I thought we should leave it alone and let nature decide. But Adam wanted to save it. He did a whole lot of research on the Web, and he set up a light bulb over a shoebox full of grass clippings, and took hourly temperature readings, adjusting the distance of the bulb from the nest, gently turning the egg every few hours. We watched and waited. To pass the time we fought terrible battles about what to name it. Adam finally won, and we called it Beverly after his grandma. Xander told him it didn't matter what its name was because it wasn't possible the egg could have survived the fall from the nest, but he wouldn't listen to her.

A week after we found the egg, Adam called us in the middle of the night, his voice high-pitched and panicky. "Come over! It's hatching!"

We ran over in our slippers and nightgowns and watched as the little bird poked its way out of the egg, its tiny little beak cracking the shell a millimeter at a time. We were so still and watchful, I found it hard to breathe. When finally Beverly emerged, skinny and oily, we looked at one another like idiots. What now?

Xander searched out some worms from Mom's garden, and we minced them up with a razor blade. The baby ate them hungrily, but kept chirruping and squeaking. It didn't seem happy.

We tried everything. Eyedroppers full of water. Cut up grasshopper guts. Nothing seemed to work.

Beverly's chirping grew weaker and weaker, so the next morning Adam's mom called the veterinarian, who called the local conservation office. Later that morning, a nice lady came by and took Beverly away. We felt like failures.

We called every day for the rest of the summer, probably driving them crazy.

Beverly survived. We even got to witness the day they let her go that autumn. Xander and I wore our Easter dresses from the year before. Adam wore a sweater and a tie. When Beverly flew away, Adam and I clapped, jumping up and down. Xander cried. That's when she still had a sensitive bone in her body. I'm pretty sure it must have been her left ulna, which she broke later that year.

"I wonder if Beverly is still alive," Adam says as he tosses his Popsicle stick under the porch stairs where we always toss them. He looks at the maple tree in front of our house as if he expects to see her there.

"That was pretty amazing, actually. The way you hatched her," Xander says quietly. She can't bring herself to look at him, but this rare compliment from Xander is not lost on Adam. He turns to her, an emotion on his face that I'm not sure I understand. All I know is that he never looks at me that way.

After a long silence, Xander lifts her eyes to Adam's, and smiles, fidgeting. Then she bolts up from the porch steps. "You guys. It's almost noon. Let's go to the bridge!" She jogs off down Olivander Street, toward the rail yard, which we nicknamed Hades because it's got so many abandoned skeletons of trains, left to rust as the sumac and thistles grow up around them. Xander turns around and yells, "Come on!" at the top of her lungs. Adam and I creakily get up to follow her. He helps me stand and keeps his hand on my back as we walk. "You okay?"

"Ugh," I explain.

"Where does she get the energy?" he mumbles.

"She sucks the blood of babies when their parents are asleep," I tell him.

He gives me a cockeyed look. "You have a dark side."

That makes me smile. Finally someone noticed.

Our town is cut in half by railroad tracks. Always at noon a big freight train rumbles through town, drowning out conversations with its whistle and bringing traffic to a complete standstill. Adam, Xander, and I like to go sit on the pedestrian overpass that runs over the tracks and watch as the train zooms underneath us.

We get there just in time. Xander sits dangling her legs while Adam and I stand next to her, watching for the train. Six sets of tracks snake underneath us, some of them littered with dormant boxcars. The trees in this part of town are thick, and the bridge we're on is so high that it looks like we're floating over a sea of leaves waving in the wind. It smells green, and you can see forever from up here.

We hear the whistle before we see the train. Adam squints at it.

"What's on it?" Xander asks.

I peer through the haze at the long line of cars approaching us. "Looks like coal?" I say, and turn to Adam.

"Lumber too," he says. He has the sharpest eyes.

"Okay, get ready!" Xander screams.

The train roars toward us, its metal heart thrumming. Adam and I stand on either side of Xander. I grab hold of the railing and stare at the engine as it surges toward us, getting bigger and bigger so quickly! Just when it looks like it's about to crash into us, Xander lifts up her shirt, screaming at the engineer: "Honk if you're a pervert!"

He couldn't have heard her, but he responds with a few sharp notes of his horn as the train booms under the bridge, car after car blurring by, its thunder shaking our bones.

When the train is gone, I say to Xander, "You don't have to flash them. They toot their horn anyway."

"It's a rush," she says, no hint of apology or shame. "You should try it next time."

I roll my eyes and look at Adam, whose thin face is alight with a smile.

He's staring at Xander like he's never seen a girl before.

NANCY

WE WALK BACK home slowly, each of us in our own thoughts. Maybe they're thinking the same thing I am. That pretty soon we'll be spread out over the East Coast. Adam will be going to NYU to study biology; Xander will probably go to MIT in Boston. And I'll be stuck here, just me and Dad in a quiet house.

Xander drives me nuts, but I still dread the day she leaves us. She's practically my whole social life. It's not that I wouldn't like to have other friends. It's just that after dealing with Xander twenty-four hours a day, I don't have the energy for anyone else.

"So, Adam," Xander says with a sly look at me as she kicks at the little bits of gravel in the gutter. "What would you say if I told you that our mom might have had an illicit affair?"

This makes me so mad that I punch her shoulder, which sends a bolt of pain through my back.

"Your mom wasn't selfish enough to do something like that," he says angrily. Adam's dad had an affair with a woman at work, another lawyer, and ran off to Boston to be with her. Adam goes to see him only four times a year, and when he comes back home he's in a bad mood for at least a week. "Believe me. Your mom wasn't the type."

"Then explain this." Xander grabs his hand and pulls him over to sit on a park bench under a sumac tree. She tells him the whole story about how we stole the documents from Mr. Blackstone, and the missing statue. "Who do women give six-thousand-dollar statues to when they die? Statues of *lovebirds?*" Xander raises her dark blond eyebrows at him and waits for his explanation.

He thinks about it, his fingers thrumming on his bony knee.

I get impatient with them both and carefully lower myself onto the ground near them. It feels wonderful to be lying down. I look up at the sky, which is speckled with tiny clouds, and I realize that it's been a very long time since I went cloud watching. That's something I did with Mom when I was very small, only I didn't know that I was supposed to be looking for shapes in the clouds. I just lay there, making up random stuff, like closets stuffed full of candy, or pirates with black eye patches. When Mom finally figured that out, that the stuff I was saying had nothing to do with watching clouds, she took me in her arms, laughing, peppering my face with kisses.

"I see why you think she might have been involved with the guy," he finally says, "but how do you know she didn't know him before she got married?"

"That's a good point," I say. "She's had that statue since before I can remember, Xander."

"When was the statue made?" Adam says.

Xander has to think about it for a minute. She closes her eyes, probably visualizing the website she'd looked at, reading it all over again. Sometimes I'm so envious of her mind that I could cry. "The website said nineteen ninety-five. Yeah. That's right. Because I remember thinking it was the same year Eric Cornell and Carl Wieman produced the first Bose-Einstein condensate."

Adam looks at me to see if I understand what she's just said. I shake my head.

"It's a model that displays quantum mechanics on a macro scale, you doofuses," she says, lisping like a nerd so we understand she's really making fun of herself.

"And when did your mom marry your dad?"

Xander probes her memory, but I'm the one who can answer this time, though I don't really want to say it. "Nineteen ninety."

"So John Phillips gave Mom the statue *after* she was married," Xander says smugly.

"After we were born," I add softly. This question had teased at the back of my mind ever since we found out about Phillips. Now it's certain. If Mom had an affair, she wasn't just cheating on Dad. She was cheating on us.

We're all quiet for a few minutes.

"Do you see?" Xander raises her eyebrows at Adam triumphantly.

"I see," Adam says impatiently, "but what I don't get, Xander, is why you're acting like you *want* it to be true."

I give Xander an accusing look.

She blusters at us. "Of—of course I don't want that!"

"Oh, yes you do," I tell her. "And I know why. Because if Mom slept around you don't have to feel so bad about doing it too. But you're going to be disappointed. Because she didn't. She wouldn't do that to us."

Xander blanches. "I don't sleep with *that* many guys."

"Okay. So you don't *sleep* with the guys," Adam says, but bites his lip immediately, seeming to regret letting the words out.

Xander pulls into herself, and I feel bad. "Xander, I think we should drop this right now," I say to her, but gently, so she'll know I'm sorry about what I said.

She looks at me with narrowed eyes. She doesn't forgive so easily.

"Actually, Zen, I'm inclined to agree with Xander," Adam says in his most reasonable-sounding adult tone. Lately he's been getting on his high horse with us. It has always been annoying to Xander, and now I find it totally enraging. "Now that you know about this Phillips guy, I don't see how you can forget about it. Besides, I'm sure you'll learn that their relationship was innocent. Then you don't have to worry about it anymore."

Xander perks up at this, but she's still mad. "I'm not a slut," she tells him, wounded.

He doesn't answer. He just lets his eyes trail down her thin white tank top and back up to her face. He raises one eyebrow.

"Bras are medieval," she tells him before getting up and flouncing away from us. We watch her go until she turns around and yells angrily, "Hey prudy-boy, is your mommy home?"

"Oh, man," he mumbles before getting up and jogging to catch up with her.

I'm not exactly thrilled either, because I know what she's about to do. She's going to ask Nancy.

When I catch up, hobbling, Adam is trying to talk sense to Xander. "Let me handle it, okay? If we don't do this tactfully, Mom'll clam up."

"You think I'm not tactful?" Xander says.

I snort. She turns around to glare at me.

"I'll ask her," Adam says. "I know how to handle her."

To this, Xander says nothing.

We climb up the front steps of Adam's house to find Nancy sitting on the porch swing reading a horror novel. All Nancy reads is horror. She loves Stephen King, and she owns every one of his novels in hardcover. They take up three whole shelves on her bookcases. Right now she's reading something by Clive Barker, biting her bottom lip with dread. We're all standing over her, waiting. When she looks up at us, she jumps in her seat.

"Jesus, Mom, didn't you hear us come up the steps?"

"Yeah," she says breathlessly. "I did." She picks up a huge tumbler of lemonade and takes a swig. "What are you guys up to today?"

"Nothing much," Adam says as he sits down in a wicker chair. She makes room on the swing for me and Xander, and we all start swinging together.

"Wheee!" Nancy says as she kicks the swing higher, holding her arms over her head like she's on a roller coaster. This is why I like

Nancy so much. She's goofy. "How are the hellions today?" Nancy asks as she pushes the swing even higher. "Starting up a rock band? Going on tour? Can I be a roadie?"

"Actually, we were just wondering if our mother was a cheeky harlot," Xander says casually.

Adam drops his head into his hands.

The swing creaks to a stop. Nancy's floppy brown hair falls in her face. Slowly she smoothes it away.

"Mom. The hellions have found something interesting about Marie, and we're just wondering." He looks at her level, so she knows he's not kidding around. "Did Marie ever mention a guy named John Phillips?"

"No," she says without even pausing to think about it. She stands up and gives Xander a freezing glare. "I've never heard the name," she says before turning on her heel and slamming through the front door.

"She's lying," Xander says flatly.

"You had to plunge right in, didn't you?" Adam yells.

Xander shrugs. "I thought she'd laugh."

"Why? It wasn't funny." He shakes his head before going in the house.

I turn on Xander. "You're the harlot, not Mom."

Xander jumps up and darts through the front door. I go into the kitchen to find her standing toe to toe with Nancy. "I'm sorry I said it that way," she pleads. "Just tell us what you know so that we don't have to think the worst!"

Nancy starts mixing herself another glass of lemonade, shaking her head, staring into the yellow liquid. "How do you know about him?" she says quietly.

Adam insinuates himself between Nancy and Xander, who he glares at until she backs away and sits down at the kitchen table.

"They found his name in some papers," he tells Nancy, using his most reasonable tone. "And she left him a very expensive item."

"The birds." Nancy lifts her eyes to his face. Her lips are trembling. She doesn't want to talk about this.

"Yes," I say. "How did you know?"

"Because I'm the one who took them to the lawyer." To Xander she says, "She didn't tell me anything about him. She just told me not to ask questions, and to deliver the statue with a letter."

Her tearful eyes pass over me and Xander. She isn't mad anymore. She's looking at us with real love. "Girls, your mother was an honorable woman."

"I know," Xander whispers.

I can't say anything, so I nod. I'm so furious with Xander for digging all this up, I could sever her carotid with a single strike. I really could.

Dojo

I LOVE THE SMELL of sweaty mats. And musty floorboards. And is that a touch of rancid turtle effluence?

According to my doctor, I can resume normal activity. I wasn't sure he remembered specifically that I'm a shotokan instructor, but I didn't remind him. Being away from the dojo has me off kilter, and I've been crazy staying at home all day long with Xander obsessing about Mom's supposedly illicit affair.

Mark is in the office, tapping on the adding machine. He's sitting with his back to me, his legs spread wide, so he looks like a Kabuki dancer. I try to sneak up behind him, but before I'm even halfway to the office he says without turning around, "Zen! Good to have you back!"

"It's good to be back!" I say, and drop to the floor to do my stretches.

Mark carefully folds up a bunch of receipts and stuffs them into an envelope. "We're well into the black this month!"

"Great!"

He sits down across from me and starts doing stretches. His dark eyes trail my limbs appraisingly. "Still stiff?"

"Yeah." I push myself a little further, working against my sprain. I feel something give and I can stretch fully, but not without pain. I try to wipe my face clean, but Mark sees my grimace.

"Are you sure you're ready for this, Zen?"

"Oh yeah."

He stops stretching and watches me quietly. I get more and more nervous under his gaze until he finally speaks. "Okay, but you're here to correct form today. You're not doing any moves."

"I can't teach without doing moves."

"You can't do shotokan with a ruined back," he says sternly. He starts stretching again, but his face remains serious. "The most important thing you can do is take care of your body, Zen. That's in shotokan and in life."

"I know that."

"You're still in pain."

His gaze is so steady, I'm not sure if he's still talking about my back or if now we're talking about Mom. Suddenly I feel weepy, and I duck my head so that my hair falls in front of my face like a blond curtain. I feel a hand on my shoulder and look up to see Mark blinking away tears. "It's been a rough year."

I nod. For a second, I'm tempted to tell him about John Phillips, because Xander's obsession has started to rub off on me, but I can't talk about it. It's too raw. And I don't want it to be real, even if I can't stop thinking about it.

"You've been very brave, Zen."

I push away my sadness, search for a topic other than Mom. I still haven't told Mark about that guy I kicked, and it really is something I should discuss with my sensei, anyway. "Mark, I had a confrontation, and I used shotokan."

He leans away from me, waiting for me to say more.

"A guy was messing with Xander, and I kicked him."

"Messing how?"

I tell him the whole story, leaving nothing out. There aren't many people in my life I can talk to like this, but with Mark, I'm completely honest. When I'm done I search his eyes, looking for the forgiveness I need from him, but I don't see it. Instead I see a distance between us as he considers my story.

"Was kicking him necessary?" he finally asks. His tone is clinical, but his eyes are grave.

I try to remember back to that night. It was important that Frank be prevented from forcing Xander into his car, but part of me wonders why I didn't try screaming first. He might have let her go. "I wasn't thinking clearly. I was scared."

"And you were angry," he says, reading me perfectly. He takes a deep breath. He has never looked at me this way before, as though he's not sure what to expect from me, like he thinks I'm dangerous.

"Yes," I say softly. "I was very angry."

"What move did you use?"

"Roundhouse kick."

"To the *head?*" he asks, surprised. "That was your *opening* move?"

"He was trying to force Xander into his car," I say to defend myself. But I sound false.

He tilts his head. "Did you call the police?"

This stops me cold. We didn't call the police. *Why* didn't we call the police?

He watches me a long time, his eyes narrow and appraising. He seems about to speak, but then we hear a reedy little voice call, "Hai!"

"Hai!" Mark says, but his eyes are on me. "We'll talk later." He rubs my back, right in the sore spot, but it feels nice. "No moves, right?"

"Okay," I say reluctantly.

The students trickle in. Nick's freckled face colors when he sees me, and he seems to want to say something, but he can't bring himself to speak. "Hey, Nick, want to help me with these mats?" I ask him.

He nods, eyes on his feet, and starts pulling the blue mats across the floor to make a large square in the middle of the room. He kicks the last one into place, and then sits down with his feet tucked under him, his eyes screwed shut.

I sit down with my knees touching his and I wait for him to

look at me. When he does, he bites on his bottom lip hard enough to turn it white.

"I know you didn't mean to hurt me."

"I thought you would be heavier!"

"It's not your fault. Honestly," I say as gently as I can. "My back was already injured, and I fell wrong. That's all."

"Okay," he whispers. His freckled forehead wrinkles up, but his shoulders relax.

Once all the kids are present, we go through the tiger warm-up routine, and then we line them up to demonstrate side-grab defense. Mark demonstrates on Nick, slowly working through the move several times, going over the points of contact.

"Okay, folks," Mark says, clapping his hands. "Break into your groups. Zen and I will show you how it's done."

I pair the kids with one another and order them to make their moves in slow motion. Everyone seems to have it pretty well except for Emily Baxter, who can't seem to straighten out her partner's arm enough to apply the proper force.

"Emily, you're not rotating his arm in the right direction," I tell her, and without thinking, I grab her partner's arm and show her the move. As I bend down, a searing pain burns through the muscles in my back and I crumble to the floor.

I feel a palm on my back, and Mark kneels beside me. "I *knew* it." He's really mad. "Lie down in my office. We'll talk after class."

I hobble to the back of the room and lie down on a yoga mat, whispering to myself over and over, "I'm okay, I'm okay, I'm okay."

My back whines with pain when I keep still, but screams if I move any part of me. All that rest has been undone. I'm sure I can look forward to another three days flat on my back, staring at the crack in my ceiling, driving myself crazy talking to Mom.

I hear the kids going through our cool-down exercises, and it makes me want to cry. The dojo has been my sanity since Mom died. I have to be able to teach. I can't do without it.

Finally I hear the mothers arrive, and the kids all put on their shoes, shouting and giggling together. I hear a quiet voice call, "Bye, Zen! I hope you feel better."

"Bye, Nick." I lift my arm to wave goodbye. Even that hurts.

Finally Mark steps over me and sits down in his chair. I don't want to have this conversation lying down, but if I try to get up, he'll see how much pain I'm really in and he might ban me for life.

He sighs loudly. From here I can see the hair in his nostrils. "Zen. You're very important to this dojo."

I smile at him. For a second, I feel relieved.

"But you're not taking proper care."

I feel the smile wipe off my face. I look away from him, toward a poster on the wall of Mount Fuji. From the corner of my eye I can see Mark shaking his head as though he doesn't know what to say next.

"I feel a very strong instinct to protect you, and I'm going to obey it."

"I'll be okay. I just need to rest."

"That's right. You do." His face is drawn with anxiety. "You know, in Eastern medicine, there's a strong belief in the mind-body connection."

"I know," I say, but wish I hadn't. I sound insolent.

"The story you told me, about kicking the man. It concerns me."

"I'm concerned too," I say, so Mark will drop it.

"And you were hurt doing a simple demonstration with the gentlest student in our class."

He pauses, waiting for me to make the connection, but I won't. I'm not going to say I let myself get hurt on purpose to make amends for kicking Frank. The guy deserved it. I set my jaw and wait for Mark to finish.

"Your back won't heal until you deal with the imbalance in your art. Then you can stand straight again."

He sounds like an episode of *Kung Fu,* and I want to laugh, but I hold it in. Mark is a cheerful person, and he's the nicest guy

I know, but he's a very strict sensei, and he takes shotokan very seriously.

"Zen. I want you to take the summer off, get your balance back."

The *summer?*

"But I can come back for class, right?" I look into his eyes pleadingly, but he's got a shield up between us.

"Come back in the fall. You'll always have a job here."

"Mark! I need this place!"

"And this place needs you. But you need to heal. And you need to find your balance again."

I try to sit up to protest, but my back feels like it's being raked with a pitchfork, and I have to lie down.

Mark raises his eyebrows, and I know there's nothing more I can say.

GETTING READY

I THOUGHT I COULD use my back as an excuse not to go to the prom, but Xander would have none of that. To make sure I followed through, she enlisted Dad, who bought in to the "it was your mother's dying wish" argument. I've been lying down for a week, but yesterday the doctor ordered me to get up and move around every day. Xander forced herself into the examination room with me so she could ask the doctor if I could go to the prom. With a tender look at me, he said, "Oh, I don't see why not, if you wear sensible shoes." Then he smiled graciously as though he'd just given me my heart's desire.

When I glared at Xander, she smiled wickedly.

The truth is, I'm going along with it, because ever since Xander started on the Prom Project she's let up about John Phillips, and it's a nice break from the gut-twisting worry that plagues me at the mere mention of his name.

Now I'm a life-size Barbie doll for Xander's friend Margot, who insisted on being my personal stylist. We're in Xander's room, where Margot smears my face with what feels like shellac before picking up a disturbingly large tube of mascara.

The skin on my face feels so stiff, I'm afraid if I smile the makeup will crack off. "Are you sure this is working for me?" I ask her.

"Stop fidgeting!" Margot whines. The mascara wand wings my forehead. "Damn it! You moved your head."

"It's hard to stay still this long!"

"That's what Zen says to her *lovers*," Xander says to Margot. "Or she would if she had any," she adds out the side of her mouth.

I let this go by. Xander has been sniping at me all evening, and the only way to deal with it is to ignore her.

Margot wipes the mascara off my forehead with her thumb and clamps her palm over my head. "Now hold still!" I can smell the garlic on her breath from the pizza she brought earlier. Her parents run the best pizza parlor in town, and she always smells like warm dough and garlic. I like Margot, but I'm not sure she's good for Xander. Since Mom died, the two of them have gotten wilder and wilder. Sometimes I wish she'd find another partner to go trolling for men with and leave my sister alone.

"Okay," Margot says, and leans back to squint at me. She nods approval and screws the mascara wand into the container. "I did a very subtle Queen of Sheba thing because that helps offset your smallish eyes. Right, Xander?"

Xander looks up from the *Maxim* she's reading. "At least she doesn't look like she has fetal alcohol syndrome anymore."

Margot shakes her head at me. "You're just jealous because Zen looks so pretty."

"Yeah, pretty in a birth defect kinda way."

I finally snap. "If you're so jealous, why did you fight so hard to make me go?"

"Who said I'm jealous?" she scoffs, and turns the magazine to get a closer look at Jessica Alba's thighs. "Do I see cellulite?" She shows the picture to Margot.

"You *wish* you did, honey," Margot says as she packs up all her makeup. She notices me slumping on Xander's squishy bed and tosses her silver evening bag at me. "Don't you want to look at yourself in the mirror?"

"Not really," I tell her. The foundation makes my skin feel like it's coated in plastic, and the lip gloss makes my mouth stick together. The dress is a little scratchy under my arms, but otherwise it's the most comfortable thing on me. Xander actually had to hold me down while Margot twisted my hair and curled it and poofed it, and then sprayed enough hairspray on me to kill all the weeds in our yard. I fully intend to strip myself of the entire outfit, even the dress, but then I stand up to humor Margot and I see myself in the mirror.

Margot is a genius. I'm a knockout.

The semi-sheer, bone-colored silk drapes over my hips in an elegant curve. The tiny sequins and rhinestones sewn into the bodice sparkle and shimmer. My shoulders are bare, which shows off my shotokan muscles and the tan that's just starting on my skin. The makeup makes my eyes look less squinty, my lips fuller, my cheekbones more pronounced, my skin milky and soft. My fine hair has been tucked into a gorgeous French knot, and wisps have been curled to form a fringe around my face.

Margot stands behind me, her hands on my arms. She has tears in her moss green eyes. "If your mother could only see you," she whispers.

Xander looks up from Jessica Alba's ass and lets an appraising eye run over me. "Yeah, Margot," she says coolly. "You did a decent job."

"I can't believe it looks so good!" I say. I put the strap from the silver bag on my shoulder and admire the way it blends so perfectly with my dress.

I'm usually a T-shirt and jeans kind of girl, but I could get used to feeling . . . what is this feeling? I guess I feel beautiful.

Xander silently snaps a picture of me. She hands me the digital camera without looking at it, and sits down at her vanity to start her own makeup. On her cheek she glues a tiny butterfly, and brushes bronzer across her cheekbones. "Anyway, you don't look twelve anymore," she says lightly.

That's as much of a compliment as I've ever gotten from her, but of course I don't thank her. "You guys are going out *again?*"

Margot won't meet my eyes, but Xander spits out, "I can do what I like. I'm almost eighteen, and there's no one to stop me."

"Just because you *can* stay out until dawn doesn't mean you *have* to." I know I sound like our mother, but someone has to, even if Mom was only pretending to be a devoted wife and mother to hide her affair with John Phillips.

The thought wrenches my stomach, and I press in to my belly with my fists to make the horrible feeling go away.

I'm not the only one who feels weird these days. Ever since we talked to Nancy about Mom, Xander has been acting strange, moodily shuffling through the house, wearing her pajamas until two in the afternoon, then going out at night with Margot, refusing to tell me where she goes. When she comes home, long after Dad has gone to bed, she smells of beer and cigarettes, and she can barely keep her eyes open. I'm used to her acting like a slut, but this new level of badness is starting to make me nervous.

Margot adjusts her minuscule skirt on her hips and turns in front of the mirror. "You ready to go?" she asks Xander.

"Yeah." Xander grabs her denim purse. To me she says, "Don't let Adam pop your cherry."

"Jesus" is all I have to say to that.

"Damn it!" Margot roots through her purse. She flips open her billfold and goes through it, card by card. "Xander, we need to swing by my house. I forgot my ID."

Xander looks at me nervously. "No problem."

"Your driver's license is right there," I say, and point to where it's poking out from behind a ten-dollar bill.

"I forgot my *other* ID." Margot winks at me.

"Let's go." Xander grabs her elbow and yanks her out of the room.

"Where are you guys going?" I'd thought they were going to parties, but they wouldn't need fake IDs for that.

Margot, ever oblivious, says, "Spirits, on Mulberry. Their bartender is so nice there!"

"Shut up, Margot! Jesus." Xander swears under her breath as she charges down the stairs ahead of us. She obviously wants to get out of here before I can ask any more questions.

Just as Xander reaches the landing, the doorbell rings. "Oh, great!" she yells. She changes course abruptly and heads for the back door.

Margot wrings her hands. "Don't tell your dad, okay?" She implores me with her eyes for a moment before following Xander out the back.

The bell rings again, and I walk down the stairs slowly, careful not to jar my back. I open the door to find Adam in a black tuxedo, holding a yellow rose, standing next to a beaming Nancy, who's huge eyes bug out when she sees me. She cups her face in her hands and squeals, "Oh, honey, you're gorgeous!"

Adam seems taken aback, and for a second he doesn't say anything, but then seems to find his voice. "Wow, Zen. You look—"

"Thanks," I interrupt, because I don't want to know what adjective he has lined up. "You too."

And he does. He's tall and well framed, with shoulders that seem broader every time I see him. The bridge of his nose is freckled slightly, which seems to heighten the pale blue of his eyes. His hair is shiny and slicked back, which makes him look perfectly clean-cut. His sideburns are a little too long, but this somehow makes him look very masculine, and uncomfortably sexy.

Widdle Adam is hot.

Dad emerges from the basement. I'm relieved to see that he's fully clothed in jeans and a sweatshirt. "Wow!" he exclaims when he sees me. "Wowie wow wow wow!"

I can feel my entire body blushing. Even the roots of my hair.

"You look—"

"Thanks, Dad." I hand him Adam's rose. "Can you put this in water please?" I say to keep him from staring. I knew I would hate this! I'm so annoyed with Mom right now, I could punch a hole in the wall. Literally.

Nancy makes Adam and me stand by the fireplace. She snaps so many pictures that my eyes ache. Then she takes my picture with Dad, and he takes her picture with me, and then they have me stand by myself. They start bickering about how I should pose, and Adam holds up his hands in a time-out signal. "Okay, folks. We have reservations so . . ."

He grabs my hand and we sprint for the car.

PROM

THE FIRST THING that happens at dinner is I drop a meatball into my lap and the tomato sauce soaks through my napkin to leave a quarter-size spot of grease on my dress. I spend fifteen minutes in the bathroom washing it out, and when I get back to our table I see that Adam has ordered me a slice of cheesecake. I hate cheesecake. I don't like the stupid cherries on top of it because they're always too cold and they hurt my teeth, and the cake itself is like plaster. I break it up with my fork to make it look like I'm eating it.

"Don't you like it?" Adam asks, worried. There's a dab of cherry sauce on his nose, but I don't know how to tell him. "I thought that all women loved cheesecake."

I could lie. Xander probably would. But lying is not my strong suit, and besides, as Mom always said, there's no dignity in lying. "Sorry. I actually can't stand cheesecake."

"Don't eat it. I shouldn't have ordered it."

"I shouldn't have dropped a meatball in my lap."

"Yeah. Watching you eat spaghetti in that dress was like watching Audrey Hepburn hock a loogie."

He's trying to make me laugh, but I feel awful. "This just isn't me."

"Getting all dressed up and stuff?" he asks as he wipes his mouth *with his tie.* "I don't know what you're talking about. It comes perfectly natural to me," he adds, deadpan, as he takes the little rose out of his lapel and uses it to pick his teeth.

I have to laugh. "You're a lunatic."

He smiles, and I notice how white and strong his teeth are. There's a little shadow of whiskers on his chin, and I realize his neck isn't as skinny as it used to be. He's starting to look like a man. I don't know how it could have happened. I've seen him every day for almost my whole life and he always looked pretty much the same to me. Not tonight, though. He's changed, and I like what it's doing to him.

I like what it does to me too.

"Come on, let's get this over with." He drops a few twenties on the table, and we leave the four-star restaurant in his mom's rusty '87 Civic with a garbage bag taped up where the rear window used to be.

When we get to the Radisson, the prom is already cranking. There are tons of people all writhing around to music I've never heard before. They all seem to know the song. Most of the girls are wearing short dresses, and I look down at my long gown, feeling like I wore the wrong thing. Adam leads me over to the punch bowl. I take a glass so that I have something to do with my hands, and I watch the people dancing.

From the mass of arms and legs, a tall boy with shiny brown hair emerges. He's holding a huge camera, and he walks up to me and Adam. "Can I take your picture for the yearbook?" he asks us.

"Oh, I don't go to this school," Adam lies, and then abandons me to go find the bathroom. He hates having his picture taken. He's like a woman that way.

The guy smiles at me nervously. "I don't remember seeing you before. Are you a senior?"

"I will be next year."

He stares at me for what seems like a long time, then hits his forehead with his hand. "You're the karate girl!"

"Yeah. I guess." I shift my weight because the ballet slippers Xander made me wear are starting to pinch my feet.

"That's right! I wanted to get a picture of you busting up a board at the talent show last year, but I ran out of film."

"It's just as well," I say.

"But that would be so great for the yearbook! It would look so cool next to some of the other sports pictures we have."

"Well, it's not like I'm on a team or anything."

"Yeah, but we don't want the football players to get *all* the attention!" He grins, very openly, and that makes me smile. "Could I get some pictures of you doing some kicks or something?"

He looks so hopeful, biting his lip, I can't say no. "I could do it next weekend, after my sister graduates, I guess."

"Okay, let me get your number." He fishes through his jacket pockets, and that's when I notice what he's wearing. It's a brown plaid leisure suit that's a little too big for him. He isn't wearing a shirt under the jacket, but around his neck is an enormous brown tie that mostly covers up his bare chest and stomach. On his feet are Birkenstock sandals. He's a wreck.

He has produced a pen and a small notebook and is waiting for me to give him my number. I realize that I've been staring.

"You've noticed my threads." He smirks.

"Yeah. Nice," I say, and then realize that it's completely obvious that I'm lying.

"I'm being subversive." He raises one eyebrow in a way that makes him seem a little cocky, a little devious. "Your number?"

Once he stows his notebook in his jacket pocket, he sticks his hand out at me. "Paul Martelli."

I shake hands with him. "Athena Vogel."

"The goddess of wisdom," he says knowingly.

"Well, I go by Zen."

"Oh yeah? Are you a Buddhist?"

"Not really."

"How do you get from Athena to Zen?"

"My sister's nickname is Xander, and I wanted a nickname too."

He nods thoughtfully. "Plus the middle syllable of Athena would begin with the Greek letter theta, which becomes Z in our alphabet. So instead of calling yourself Then, you're Zen. Very cool."

My mouth drops open. "You're the first person who has ever made that connection."

"I like that kind of stuff, that's all," he says just as Adam comes back from the bathroom. Paul's demeanor changes, and he gives Adam a simple nod before disappearing behind a swath of dancers.

"Want to dance?" Adam asks just as the music shifts. It's a slow song, and it doesn't sound like something that would make me look like a complete fool, or send me to the emergency room with a slipped disk, so I nod and let him lead me onto the dance floor.

It's strange to put my arms around Adam's neck, because he's so much more solid than I thought he'd feel. His hands are large and warm on my back, and I notice myself getting a little nervous, but it's a good kind of nervous. Adam is looking over my shoulder, sort of staring into space. I can't tell if he feels nervous in the same way I do or not. Somehow, when I feel this way, it becomes so hard to read people.

"So, Zen," Adam says in my ear. "I've been a little worried."

I feel a cloak of disappointment fall over my shoulders, and it makes me sag. "About Xander?"

"Don't you think she's acting wild lately, even for her?"

I nod because I feel too sad to talk. Even when she isn't here, Xander dominates his thoughts. Usually I like how she draws the attention to herself because I hate being noticed. But tonight, wearing this dress, with my arms around Adam, I want to be the one who glows.

"Do you think it would help if I talked to her?" Adam says.

"Oh, come on," I say, annoyance laced through my voice. I feel like the answer to this question is so obvious that he probably already knows it. And that makes me wonder why he's brought up Xander at all. Just to have something to talk to me about, because she's the one thing we have in common? Or is he trying to distance himself from me? Or is it that he can't stop thinking about her, even now?

"I mean, the other day with the train . . ." he stutters.

"When she flashed the engineer?"

"Yeah. That was . . ."

"You liked it. Don't pretend you didn't."

That shuts him up. He readjusts his hands on my back.

"It's not that I liked it. It's just . . ." His shoulders stiffen under my arms, and I glance at his face to see that it's gone blank, as though all his muscles have tightened. "Zen, I'm afraid she's going to get hurt." He pulls away to look at me, his mouth tight. He's scared. "I think she *wants* to get hurt, Zen."

We sway slowly under the prism of lights while I think about what he's said.

Xander has always been careless. When we were kids she used to rollerblade down the biggest hill in our town, screaming the whole way. I'd go down it too, but I'd put on the brakes every so often. Not Xander. She pointed her toes straight downhill and coasted as fast as she could go. When Mom got on her case about it, she'd pout, muttering that it's too hard to have any fun if you're scared all the time. I always secretly agreed with her. But now it doesn't really seem like Xander's having that much fun.

I glance at Adam, and I see he's watching me, his eyes troubled. Suddenly he's Widdle Adam from across the street again, and I'm Zen Vogel with the skinny legs and the innocent face. What he's said makes me worry even more, because now that the idea has entered my mind, I think he might be right.

Xander's Bar

We leave the prom kind of early, trailing out with some kids who are headed to an after party in a hotel room somewhere. One of the girls, a senior, screams out her car window, "Premarital sex!" and laughs maniacally.

Adam shakes his head; I roll my eyes, but I feel strangely empty. Prom night is when lots of girls lose their virginity, and I know that's not going to happen tonight, and definitely never with Adam. I didn't come to the prom hoping to have sex with anyone, but for the first time, I wonder why I'm the only teenage girl in America who isn't chasing after boys. Maybe Xander's right. Maybe something is wrong with me. Mom always said it's just that I'm too cerebral, but I can't help wondering if I really *am* frigid like Xander says.

Adam drives in silence to the bar where Xander and Margot are supposed to be. I don't really want tonight to be about Xander, but when I told Adam about her fake ID he got really worried and insisted on checking out the place. "I just want to make sure she's safe," he said.

She. No thought for Margot.

I study his profile, the way he's peering into the dark street as he drives, licking his lips, his brow tense. Everything about him seems strained. I wonder if I were at a bar, would he come looking for me? Would he be this worried?

"That must be the place," he says, and slows down to park.

The bar shares a parking lot with a liquor store and a check-cashing place. Across the road is a strip joint.

"This street reminds me of every Tarantino movie I've ever seen," Adam says through his teeth. He watches the door as a large, leaning man stumbles through it, keys in hand. He lurches to his truck, burping loudly. After him comes a very small woman wearing a tight-fitting denim vest. "Give me those damn keys, Harvey, I mean it!" she bellows as she yanks them out of his hand. He sort of crawls, sort of falls into the truck and she crawls in after him, swearing loudly.

"Charming," Adam says as he takes off his jacket.

"What are you doing?"

"You wait here. I'm going to see what she's up to." He pulls his tie off over his head and unclips his cummerbund. "Do I look like a kid who just left the prom?"

I grudgingly look him over. His normally springy hair is slicked back, and his shadow of whiskers adds years to his face. "You'll pass."

He points his finger in my face and says sternly, "You stay here."

I hit his hand away and fold my arms over my front. I expect to hear the car door close, but instead I hear, "I'm sorry, Zen."

I turn to look at him. He's leaning into the car, his face solemn and sad. His eyes are too honest. He isn't just apologizing for talking to me like I'm a child, or for leaving me alone in the car. He's apologizing for preferring Xander to me. I've known him long enough to see that.

I'm furious that he would expose me like this, and I turn away from him, twice as angry as I was before. He can have her, as far as I'm concerned. Let someone else baby-sit her for a change. I'd love the vacation.

He slowly walks to the door of the bar. The steady way he's stepping over the gravel shows how scared he really is. He opens the door, and a loud swatch of guitar music sails into the night. The door closes behind him, and I'm all alone in the quiet.

I can hear crickets chirping, and every so often a frog's throaty call. We must be near the river that runs through town along the railroad tracks until they veer north. The door opens, and I see two youngish guys come out. One of them says, "I knew she wasn't twenty-one." I peek into the window to see Xander fast-talking a tall, pretty woman who is holding up a phone and pointing to the door.

The door swings open again. Margot stomps out in her sequined platform sandals. When she sees me, she marches over and opens the rear door so hard, the car jiggles. "Thanks a lot, Zen. And after I did all your makeup!"

"What happened?" I try to sound surprised.

"Adam told the bartender we had fake IDs!" Margot yanks her crystal combs out of my hair, none too gently. "Where did he get *that* idea?"

"He said he just wanted to check the place out."

"You shouldn't have told him where we were! You know how protective he is of Xander!" She angrily shoves the crystal combs in her own huge hair, which swallows them up. "He's totally in love with her!"

I don't say anything to this. It makes me feel shaky. I just want to get out of here.

The door slams open and Xander flounces out. She's heading for our hatchback, but when she sees Margot sitting in the back seat of Adam's car, she makes two fists and stomps over to us. "What the hell are you doing in his car?" she slurs, her face twisted in a nasty scowl at Margot.

"I don't want to drive with you," Margot says to her. "You're drunk."

"I'm not!" Xander says. She doesn't even look at me. She only ignores me like this when she's insane with fury.

Adam comes out, tucking his wallet into his back pocket. "I paid your enormous tab," he tells Xander angrily. "Get in my car."

"Go to hell," Xander says, and takes off toward the hatchback.

Adam marches up to her and grabs her elbow. She jerks away from him. "Who appointed you my daddy?"

He doesn't say anything, just grimly clamps his arms around her and lifts her toward his mom's car. She kicks at his legs, catching his shin. He yells and lets go of her before falling down. She takes off at a run, laughing wildly.

"Oh, man, she's really lost it now," Margot says.

"You're just catching on to that fact?" I spit at her.

"Hey, don't yell at me! She's not my responsibility!"

"No, just your best friend!"

I turn to see that Adam is holding Xander around the waist. She's bent away from him, laughing her ass off. "Let go of me!" she keeps trying to say, but she can't form the words without laughing right through them.

Adam leans his head on her back and yells, "No!" He's laughing too now. "Come on!" he wheezes. "Get in my car!"

Xander relaxes. "Okay, fine. You're right. I'll get in your car, just let me stand up."

Adam doesn't want to let her go at first, but slowly he releases his grip on her waist. As soon as his guard lets down, she bursts out of his hold and sprints for her car, yelling, "I won! You're a loser, Adam Little!" She pulls on the handle of the car door, but it doesn't open. She feels around her pockets for the keys, and looks at Adam, sheepish. "Oh shit."

Just then the door opens and the bartender appears. She gives Xander a mean-eyed look before throwing her denim purse at her. "Don't come back," she says, and slams the door for emphasis.

Xander looks at Adam, who puts his hands on his hips, tapping his toe.

Head down, she walks over to her purse, picks it up, dusts it off, and gets in the back seat behind me. Before Adam can get in, I feel a sharp pinch on my shoulder.

"Ow!" I squeal. I forget my back and twist around to try to hit her, but the searing pain stops me and I have to sit very still and try to catch my breath.

"Oh, that was an accident, I'm so sorry!" Xander says as she pinches me even harder.

Adam gets in. "Everyone put on their seat belts."

"Or Adam here won't win Fuddy Duddy of the Year," Xander clucks.

The drive is quiet for a few blocks. Too quiet.

"Ow!" Margot suddenly yells, and I turn to see her rubbing her shoulder. "What's *that* for?!"

"That's for telling her where we'd be tonight!" Xander yells.

The rest of the way home, Xander pinches us all at random until Adam finally tells her he'll drop her off in the middle of nowhere if she doesn't quit it.

She stops pinching him and Margot.

I am not so lucky.

Aunt Doris

I'M LEANED BACK in the car seat, trying to find a position that won't hurt. Through the window I watch the treetops zoom by. There's only one little white cloud in the whole sky, and I wonder about it. Where did that cloud come from? Why is it all alone?

Xander and I are on our way to see Aunt Doris in Brattleboro, Vermont, which is about three hours away from us. She talked Dad into it, saying the trip could be her graduation present. He let us go, even though we just saw Doris at Xander's immensely long, immensely boring graduation. It was one long line after another. A line waiting to get into the gymnasium. Then a line to get out. A line to pick up Xander's diploma. A line to get our picture taken by the professional photographer. It was like Disneyland without the plushies.

I'm just glad the school year is over with.

The drive is pretty, through long rolling hills and lots of beautiful green pastures with black and white cows in them. Above us I see a formation of geese returning for the summer. They fly right through the little white cloud. They don't even seem to notice it.

We get to the section of the highway that's almost totally covered with leafy trees, and I roll down the window to let the green smell in.

"Close it," Xander snaps.

"No."

"It's whipping my hair in my face."

"So?"

"You still owe me for telling Adam about my bar. So I think you can close the damn window."

"You're mistaken. I owe you nothing. And it's not your bar."

"It was. Now I have no ID and no place to go!"

"Poor little hussy."

"Frigid little virgin."

"Adam and I were just looking out for you. Someone has to."

"Adam and you can make out with each other in a minefield for all I care."

I study her profile. I know she can feel me looking at her, but she's too stubborn to give me even a fleeting glance.

"You know, Adam wouldn't act like your jailor if you didn't act like such a delinquent."

"I'm not acting."

I root through the bag of junk food that I bought during our last stop for gas. I unwrap a package of Ding Dongs and hand one to Xander to stuff in her mouth.

"So you should be the one to bring it up with Doris," Xander says through a mouthful of mushed-up cake as she blithely passes a semi.

"Bring what up?" I say just to irritate her.

"John Phillips!" she yells, spitting chocolate through her gross teeth.

Aunt Doris isn't very vulnerable to Xander's tactics. She responds better to straightforward earnestness, which is my forte. "Leave me alone with her tonight."

"Gotcha."

I wish Xander and I had never stolen Mom's file from Mr. Blackstone, and I wish we had never heard of John Phillips. Now that we know about him, I can't sleep, I have no appetite, and I hardly want to talk to Mom in my mind anymore. I need to know, but not for the same reasons as Xander. I want Mom to be exonerated so I can go back to thinking of her as a devoted wife and mother who would never do anything to hurt her family.

Xander takes the exit off the highway to Brattleboro, which is a little mountain town tucked between green mounds of trees. You can't see very far in Brattleboro because there are too many leaves in the way. In the winter, when the trees are bare, Brattleboro transforms into a completely different town, and you can see for miles, all the way to the hills that surround the little valley. But now the valley is so close, it feels like we're in a big green room.

We hang a left onto Stump Road and follow it up between the trees. We pass by the neighbor's place, where we see a new foal with its mother, both of them brown and shining in the sun. Their glossy coats remind me of the yearbook photographer's shiny hair. What was his name? Paul. He was supposed to take my picture this weekend, but he never called.

Aunt Doris is sitting on her porch waiting for us with Blue, her slobbery yellow Lab. She lives in our grandparents' old farmhouse. She moved in with Grandma after Grandpa died in his sleep eight years ago. Doris took care of Grandma until she died of missing him, two years later. Then Aunt Doris just stayed in the house, and I can't imagine her anywhere else.

Xander honks when we pull into the gravel parking lot, and Doris bolts down the stairs and makes a run for our car. Aunt Doris is a little on the chubby side, but she can move like the wind. Blue follows, loping over, barking deep from his chest.

"How're my girls!" She jumps up and down while she waits for Xander and me to get out. I stand up carefully. After three hours in the car, my back is stiff.

Doris seems confused about which of us to hug first, so she holds her arms out to us both and hugs us at the same time. "It's wonderful to see such fresh faces!" she cries.

Even though she is ten years older than my mother was, Aunt Doris looks younger than she is, probably because she grows her own vegetables and she doesn't eat meat or cheese. She was a teenager in the seventies when people were still hippies. She looks like a hippie, with her long gray hair and brown skin, and her turquoise jewelry and flowing skirts and cotton tunics. She has about twenty sterling silver rings that she wears all at once on her fingers and toes, and you can hear her wherever she goes because her dozens of silver bangles rattle as she walks.

I kneel down to pet Blue, who slobbers all over my arms, while Doris interrogates Xander. "So! Is it MIT or Caltech?"

"I don't know," Xander says. Her eyes dart over Doris nervously. Everyone is asking her this question these days, and she doesn't like it. I don't know why she's taking so long to decide.

"Don't you have to commit to them sometime soon?" Doris tosses a hunk of hair out of her face.

"I have to give them my final decision on Monday," Xander says. Her thin hand covers her stomach.

Doris wraps an arm around Xander and holds a hand out to me until I take it. "Want to see what I've been working on lately?" She pulls us into her warm living room.

Inside, all the windows are open because Aunt Doris doesn't believe in air conditioning, but it's all right because even though it's a hot day, it somehow feels comfortable. We follow her through the living room of furniture slipcovered in light blue denim. Lining the walls are shelves full of hundreds of books and magazines stacked every which way. Her dining table is littered with scraps of fabric, a beading kit, small piles of the doll clothes she sews, and for reasons I do not want to contemplate, three mousetraps.

We walk through the kitchen to the back sunroom, which is Doris's studio. There are dozens of paintings leaning against the walls and stacked on the floor, and we have to weave through them to get to the canvases Doris wants us to see.

Xander gasps.

Aunt Doris has done a portrait series of Mom, at all ages, all based on family photographs that I recognize. The portrait of Mom as a little girl is based on a picture we have of her holding a sand bucket on the beach in Nantucket, but instead Aunt Doris has placed her on the surface of the moon, waving and laughing as the rising Earth glows blue over her shoulder. In another one she's a teenager suspended on a bed of clouds tinged pink by the dusk. In the third she's a young college student wearing amber beads and sitting on the rings of Saturn. In the fourth, she is a bride gliding over the surface of a comet. In the last one, she is sitting in her favorite wicker chair on the porch of our house, on Earth. In this portrait she already looks a little sick, but still beautiful, and serene.

"I'm calling the series Marie, Forever," Aunt Doris whispers.

I feel tears hitting my chest before I realize I'm crying. I look at Xander, whose face is motionless, though I can tell there's an ocean of feeling churning inside of her. Doris's eyes are red and moist, and she says, "Maybe I should have warned you. I didn't know how to show you."

"I love them," I tell her. "Please don't sell them."

"Oh, no. I never will," she says, studying the last one. "These are how I've been grieving."

Xander looks at her, surprised, as if she never thought there could be a *way* to grieve. I guess we all have our ways, though. Dad has pulled himself out of the world and spends most of his time in the basement in his new bedroom because he can't bear to be in the bedroom that he shared with Mom for so many years. Xander has turned into a wildcat. I sit in Mom's old room, in the chair she sat in to watch the birds outside her window, and drink too much mint tea while talking to her in my head.

Aunt Doris's way seems like the best.

We spend the afternoon walking the property line along the crumbling fence that Grandpa put up when he first bought the place. Blue runs back and forth, stopping only to slobber on our hands before bounding off after a squirrel. I should take life-loving lessons from him.

We stop at the neighbor's fence to beckon the little brown foal, who stands in the middle of her green field, blinking her enormous eyes at us. Her mother saunters over, head down, and takes the carrot offered by Doris. Once the foal sees that, she trots up to us and takes a piece of apple in her big floppy lips. Doris smiles. "Apples are better for the babies. Softer." She threads her fingers through the foal's mane, seeming to be living inside that silky feeling. I reach my hand out to feel for myself, but the foal backs off and trots away. "She's still shy," Doris says. "It took two weeks before she'd let me touch her."

"Poor thing," Xander says, mournful.

Doris looks at Xander quizzically, which is probably how I'm looking at her too. I don't know why she feels sorry for the little foal, who seems perfectly happy not to be touched.

When evening falls we go back to the house and eat what Aunt Doris calls a ploughman's supper of crusty bread, hummus, bean salad, fresh greens, sliced tomatoes, and honey cakes for dessert. It's delicious. I don't even miss meat when I'm staying with Doris.

Once we're all three of us stuffed and leaning back in our chairs, Xander raises her eyebrows at me and gets up from the table. "I think Venus is rising this time of year. I'm going to go check." She wanders out the front door and onto the porch, stretching herself toward the night.

Doris levels her steady gaze on me. "How are you, Athena?"

"Not so great, I guess." I know better than to pretend with Doris.

"What's going on? I know this isn't just a social visit. I can sense it." She squints through the front windows at Xander, who seems to feel her gaze and slowly walks off the porch and into the dark front yard.

"Are you the one?" I ask her, and wait until her eyes land on me. "Who's sending the letters?"

"What letters?" she leans forward, instantly intrigued. I can tell already, she doesn't even know about them.

"Mom is having someone send Xander and me letters for certain occasions. We've each gotten them, one right after she died, a video at Christmas, and a second letter on Mother's Day."

"That sounds like my Marie." There's such longing in her voice, I have to look away. We're both quiet, in our own thoughts, but then I hear her sniff. "No, hon, I'm sorry it isn't me. I expect she thought I'd be too disorganized to do it properly."

I look around the jumbled room, which I've always loved because it feels so homey, and I realize that Doris is probably the last person Mom would put in charge of her letters. She would probably lose them in one of her many piles.

Doris cocks her head. "Why would you want to find this person anyway? Why not just let the letters come?"

"Xander's the one who wants to know." I stop. I feel like I'd be betraying my mother by asking what we really came for. But I need to find out the truth about John Phillips. If I don't, I'll feel like I never really knew Mom, and that is too painful to live with. "We found out some stuff, and we're—confused."

Doris's bangles rattle as she crosses her arms. "What stuff?"

"Mom seemed to have some kind of friendship with a man named John Phillips."

She shakes her head. "No, I don't think so, honey. I've never heard that name. And your mother always told me everything."

I study her face. There isn't anything about her round eyes or her full cheeks that suggests she might be lying. She doesn't even seem concerned.

"She left him one of her bird statues. The lovebirds."

Doris's eyes freeze on me. "Now, that's odd. I thought she wanted you girls to have all of them."

It's on the tip of my tongue to tell her the final details, that the statue was worth six thousand dollars, and that he couldn't have given it to her until well after Xander and I were born, but I stop myself. Why should Aunt Doris feel as troubled as I've been feeling?

I can see, though, that she's already troubled.

"That's *very* odd," Doris says again. "I can't imagine why she'd give it away. She loved that statue."

We're both silent, mirroring each other's worried faces.

"Your mother always told me everything," Doris says again, leaning back, thinking. "But there was one period in her life when she seemed to pull away from me, when she was in graduate school with your father. I wouldn't hear from her for weeks, and when I'd ask her how she was, she'd say she was fine in a very distant way, and she'd only talk about her classes." Doris's face darkens, and she says, her voice throaty, "If she was hiding a man from me, that would have been when she did it."

"Why would she hide a man?" I ask, because I desperately want Doris to come up with an explanation other than the one I'm imagining. That not only was Mom cheating on Dad, but it started way back in graduate school. Mom might have cheated on us for years and years. I try to dismiss the thought, but I can't. Everything we find out just makes it worse and worse.

Doris shakes her head. "The only reason she ever hid anything from me was because she was ashamed."

GETTING HIGH WITH XANDER

XANDER STILL HASN'T COME BACK, so Doris and I do the dishes alone, which takes a long time because she doesn't have a dishwasher. I kind of like doing dishes the old-fashioned way because the warm water feels good on my hands.

"Hand me that blue dish." Doris nods toward the table behind her.

I give her the one with the lilacs painted on the rim.

"No, the other one," she tells me, and points toward the dish that held the honey cakes. It's painted with blue cornflowers.

Doris likes to wash her dishes in a particular order because she displays them in her china cabinet in a certain way. She is sloppy about everything except her dishes, probably because she's spent such a long time collecting them. They're all different because she buys them one at a time at garage sales. They're each hand-painted with a beautiful pattern, and she chooses them carefully. There's something very comforting about eating on an antique plate. It reminds me of how many people there really are, and how many there have been, and how many of them must have eaten their dinner from this same plate. Each plate is like looking at a different side of forever.

Xander likes Doris's plates as much as I do, but she always eats from the same one. It's a green and white plate, and on it is a painted picture of ducks flying, and a hunter with his dog, watching them.

She likes it because the hunter isn't shooting at the ducks. He's letting them fly away, holding his gun down at his side.

"Well, honey," Doris says, stretching to put away the last plate in her cupboard before closing the door. "Blue is hanging his head, and that always makes me sleepy." I look over at Blue, who is panting in the corner, his eyelids sagging over eyes that are glued to Aunt Doris. "Stay up as long as you want."

She brushes her hand over my hair and smiles into my eyes.

Even if I can't ever see Mom again, at least I have Aunt Doris, who loves me almost as much as Mom did.

I don't feel sleepy yet, so I'm looking over Doris's bookshelves for some bedtime reading when I hear the screen door creak open. Xander is standing in the doorway, a devilish smile on her lips. In her hand she's holding a pipe of some kind. "Ever dabbled in wacky tobacky?"

I stare at her, confused. She cocks her head, and I follow her out onto the porch.

"What is that?" I ask her.

"Oh don't tell me you're surprised to know Doris smokes weed! Hell, she probably grows her own!"

I can't help the shock on my face.

"Come on, Zen!" Xander whispers. "The woman wears a *mood ring* for god's sake! Of course she tokes!"

"Where did you find it?"

"Upstairs. She had the pipe in plain view on her dresser!"

"But, you've been outside the whole time!"

"I climbed up the trellis and snuck in through her bedroom window while you were doing the dishes. Blue sucks as a watchdog."

She walks across the lawn and opens the car door, beckoning me to get in. She pulls a lighter out of her hip pocket and holds it over the pipe. The fuzzy stuff in the center starts to glow red, and Xander inhales deeply. Through a closed throat she says, "Do it like that."

I look at the pipe a second before taking it from her. It feels warm and heavy in my hand. I pause to wonder whether I really want to do this. "What if I get addicted?"

"It's weed! Not crack," Xander wheedles. "Beer will mess you up worse."

I have to admit to a certain curiosity, so I raise the pipe to my lips and draw in deeply.

I feel like I just inhaled burning-hot nerve gas. All the blood rushes to my eyes and I cough and cough until I feel like I'm going to have a stroke. Xander taps my back, saying, "It's harsh the first time, but you get used to it."

"I'll never get used to that!" I say when I can finally speak.

Xander roots through the grocery bag on the seat between us and pulls out a bottle of water. "Drink."

The cold is wonderful against my throat, which feels like I swallowed a mouthful of sparks. I drink until my lungs feel almost normal, and then I lean back and close my eyes. "That was awful."

"Next time it's brownies for you." Xander smiles and takes another hit. She doesn't even cough, and I wonder how often she does this.

"You know, that's not good for your brain."

"I have IQ points to spare." She looks around Doris's yard, still smiling to herself. "You know, I really love this place. Do you think Doris will leave it to us?" She wiggles her eyebrows devilishly.

"Mercenary," I say. I notice a muffled feeling creep over my brain. I blink my eyes, and it seems like suddenly I can see very clearly, even in the dark. "I don't want Doris to die," I say from far away, and add for good measure, "I think I'm high."

"That's no lie," she says.

I chuckle. "I feel like I could fly."

"Don't even try."

"There's a sty in your eye."

"Your vagina is dry."

"You think you're so sly . . . but you're not," I sputter, and burst into hysterical laughter. A tiny part of my brain questions why I think this is so hilarious.

Xander is snorting and holding her stomach. She has the ugliest, most obscene laugh of anyone I know. But I love it.

We sit there giggling until we run out of breath, and we trade swigs of water until it's all gone, then Xander tears into a bag of Doritos. "You know, you're more fun without those numchucks you keep up your ass."

"It's a throwing star, if you *must* know."

She spits out corn chips, she laughs so hard.

We finish all the Doritos and the other package of Ding Dongs, then go back into the house and sink into Doris's furniture like a couple of boneless worms.

"That's good weed," Xander says. "Doris is connected!"

"She's totally going to find out," I say, and this becomes the most horrible thought I've ever had. "Oh my god, she'll never forgive us! We have to put the pipe back right away!" I look out the window, searching for the police who must be creeping up to the house.

"Calm down, you're paranoid. It'll be fine." Xander leans back in the big fluffy chair, staring up at the tin ceiling, which is covered with chipped white paint. Her breathing seems to even out, and I think she's falling asleep, but then she murmurs, "I wonder what Adam is doing right now."

This gets my attention, and suddenly I'm awake, though I hadn't noticed I was falling asleep. "Adam? Why do you bring him up?"

She pinches the bridge of her nose and screws her eyes shut. "I don't know. I'm high."

I roll my head against the back of my chair and look at her. She seems so small, lying there like that. For once she's not darting around, just out of my reach, challenging me, egging me on. She's still, letting her mind wander where it will. Interesting that it should go to Adam.

"You love him, don't you?" I say. There's a little hint of despair in my voice, but I find now that I've said it out loud, it's not such a painful truth to face up to.

Xander pretends to misunderstand. "Of course. He's our oldest friend." Her voice is too light, too casual.

"You know what I mean. You do, don't you?"

She sniffs. Her eyes travel over the chipped paint on the ceiling, and then drop to the crack in the plaster wall. "It doesn't matter anyway," she says.

I've never heard her sound so thick, so weighted down.

"Why doesn't it matter?"

"Because. After this summer, that's it. We're leaving. And it'll never be the same again." She says this like it's something she accepted a long time ago.

But I hate it. I hate what she's saying.

I watch a moth fluttering in the corner of the room, in the circle of light cast up by the lamp on the side table. What does the moth want, beating against the walls like that? Is it trying to get out?

Or is beating itself the whole point?

"I miss Mom." The words seem to come out of the air, and I'm not sure who said them, me or Xander.

I look at her. Her eyes are closed, but her face is drawn in grief. Maybe she said it.

"I do too," I tell her, every strand of my voice aching for Mom. I wish so much there was some bridge I could walk across, like the railroad bridge, and I could get to the other side of wherever she is so that I could see her again.

If I ever had a really bad day, Mom and I would walk downtown and share a hot fudge sundae with nuts and whipped cream, and we'd talk about it. Being in the ice cream parlor, surrounded by the red and white striped wallpaper, and the chrome chairs, listening to the oldies station that they played there, I always cheered up. After she died, I was so sad that I went to get a sundae and I ate it all alone. It made me feel twice as miserable as I did before, and I haven't gone back there since.

Xander jerks awake all of a sudden. "What did Doris say?" Her voice sounds different, like she's back to the old Xander.

It takes me a second to switch gears, but I catch up. "She doesn't know John Phillips, but she thinks if Mom ever dated him it would have been during graduate school."

"But Mom and Dad always said that's when *they* were dating." She rubs her thumbs into her eyes and yawns. "I suppose Doris isn't the one sending the letters?"

"Right. How did you know?"

"I figured. When I found the pot I realized Doris would be a terrible person to send them. She's too flaky."

This makes me worry. "She's not a burnout, is she?"

"God, Zen, she's the most vibrant person we know!"

This is true, but I do wonder if Doris didn't smoke pot, would her paintings be hanging in New York galleries instead of Vermont coffeehouses?

Does that really matter?

I think about this until I fall asleep on the sofa, imagining portraits of my mother covering tall white walls.

After Toking

"I'm very disappointed."

"I know. I'm sorry. I shouldn't have smoked the pot."

"Now you're going to be a stoner burnout with tooth decay and dreadlocks."

"Would you feel better if I told you I didn't like it that much?"

"You didn't?"

"No. I couldn't concentrate on anything, and I didn't like the way my mind wandered. It made me anxious."

"Well, that's good. It's not as harmless as the potheads would have you believe. I think it's why Doris never got married. Scared off all the right guys, and she was always so high, she let all the wrong ones stick around too long."

"She seems to like being single."

"She resigned herself to it a long time ago."

"Does Xander smoke it a lot?"

"With her, I'm more worried about alcohol. And boys."

"Do you think she's in love with Adam?"

"Of course she is, honey. So are you."

"But it's different with me. I think I have more like a crush. There's something more serious about the way she feels about him."

"Well, I hope that's true. He'd be good for her."

I get a sudden suspicion. I can't believe I didn't see it before. "Did you make me go to the prom with Adam to make Xander jealous?"

AMY KATHLEEN RYAN ❄ 104

Her only response is a self-satisfied chuckle.

I open one eye to see Xander lying in the recliner across the room from me. She's snoring softly. I can hear the song of crickets through the screen door, and cicadas, and I remember something Adam once told me, that they make that sound because they're looking for a mate.

"Mom?"

"It's none of your business."

"Who is John Phillips?"

"Ancient history."

"I want to know. Did you have an affair with him?"

She's silent. It's an angry silence.

"You can't blame us for wanting to know!"

"Everybody has secrets, Zen. Especially parents."

"Did you have an affair, Mom? Did you cheat on us? How could you do that?"

"You're jumping to conclusions."

"Did you love him?"

She's silent for a long time. I imagine her floating through the dust particles that hover between Doris's paintings. There's a whisper in the air, and there's such longing in the word that I almost hear it with my ears, not just my mind:

Yes.

WAFFLES AND LETTERS

"I SEE YOU'VE FOUND MY STASH," I hear said before I open my eyes. Doris is holding her pipe, standing over us, lips pursed. I wouldn't say she's mad so much as *pretending* to be mad.

"You're a terrible influence," Xander informs her. It takes her several tries to sit up. Doris plunks down on the ottoman just as Xander manages to heave her legs off it.

"I'm going to pretend I don't know about this, considering I don't exactly have the moral authority to lecture you."

"Can we have waffles for breakfast?" Xander asks, giving Doris her goofiest grin.

Wincing, Doris waves her hand in front of her nose. "After you brush your teeth. Twice. And shower. Geez. You smell like a bong."

I inch myself off the couch, moving carefully. I should not have slept here. My back feels like it has steel pins jammed into it.

Once we're cleaned up, we drive into the village to have breakfast at Willy's, a tiny bakery that shares a building with a little grocery store. It looks junky from the outside because of the flickering neon sign and the empty milk crates that line the sidewalk, but once you get inside, it's airy and pretty. The windows are covered in yellow checked curtains, and the tables are ancient farmhouse antiques whose wood has been rubbed smooth by decades of damp rags. We sit in the corner by the window, not even bothering to look at the menus because we already know what we want—waffles with real

Vermont maple syrup, scrambled eggs, and a bowl of blueberries on the side.

"So, Aunt Doris," Xander says through a mouthful of berries, "how can we find out who John Phillips is?"

"Did you do a search for the guy on the, um . . . Internet?"

Xander nods. "There are only about five thousand John Phillipses in the United States."

Doris sips at her coffee, her expression very serious. She holds the mug with both hands, warming her knuckles against the thick stoneware. "Are you sure you want to know, Xander? Really?"

"Do you think Mom was—" I begin, but I can't finish.

"I don't think so, sweetie," Doris says. She reaches across the table and pats my hand. "She loved your father very much. I know she did."

"Then why would she hide this guy from us?" Xander cuts an enormous bite of waffle and edges it into her mouth.

"I can't fathom." She sets her mug down on the table. "But I do feel that if Marie wanted to keep him a secret, we should respect her privacy."

Xander swallows, audibly, and looks at me. For once nothing in her manner is playful. I fold my hands in my lap. Suddenly my waffle looks inedible, and my stomach feels like it's full of mud. I imagine Mom slipping out the door of our house, leaving Xander and me with some babysitter, or, worse, with Grandma, while she runs off to have a tryst with some stranger. It makes me want to throw up.

Doris sips at her coffee, looking back and forth between Xander and me. "You girls will always wonder, won't you?"

Xander nods. I keep my silence.

"Well, your grandma kept some of your mother's notebooks and papers from graduate school. Maybe we'll find something up there," Doris says, but she seems very worried. "I just want you to remember, girls, that she was still your mother, whatever we find out."

"I know," I say, silently fuming at Xander. Just like the robin's egg we found all those years ago, she wants to crack everything open and look at what's inside. She couldn't see that the egg was beautiful as it was.

We finish up breakfast and drive through the town. Main Street is full of little kids playing, and parents standing around in groups talking. We stop at a red light, and I watch a very tall man and a short blond woman walking their puffy little white dog. He prances along ahead of them, stopping to sniff at something, and then jumps ahead again. The man puts his arms around the woman's shoulders and whispers something in her ear. She laughs loudly the way Mom used to, but that's not why I feel so empty watching them. They have something that I don't have. They have something that Adam wants to have with Xander. No one has ever wanted to have it with me. And until very recently, I never really wanted it either.

Or maybe I just didn't know I wanted it.

Once we get back to Doris's house, we climb the stairs to her sweltering attic and we start sifting through boxes of old stuff. *Detritus* is what Doris calls it. It turns out to be a treasure trove of leftovers from Mom's life. We lose two hours looking through Mom's papers from high school. It's so strange to see her writing as a girl. It was rounder, more flowery, like she was still trying to figure out who she was on paper. For a while she even dotted her *i*'s with little check marks. Xander laughs, but it gives me a deep ache. Mom was so many people. Once she was a teenager, like I am now. Then she was a young woman, dating men, hanging out with friends. Then she was a wife. And then she was a mother. John Phillips knew her as one of these people. Or maybe, for him, she was a different person altogether. Someone I didn't know.

Finally Doris finds the box full of Mom's notes from graduate school. We sift through piles of typed essays and spiral notebooks full of scratched notes about James Fenimore Cooper, Willa Cather,

Emily Brontë, Edgar Allan Poe. I pick up a term paper she wrote about a poem by John Keats called "Ode to a Nightingale" and start reading. The language is so technical, full of words like *chiaroscuro* and *pentameter,* I'm lost before I finish the first paragraph. I skip to the last page and see that she got an A, and a note from her professor that said, "Not only does this essay show a depth of thinking beyond what I'd expect from a master's candidate, but it is written with a fresh and engaging voice. You should consider applying to a Ph.D. program, Marie. You clearly have a talent for criticism."

I had no idea Mom was doing so well in graduate school. She always acted like Dad was the star. But Mom was very smart. Her professor thought so, anyway. Why did she downplay her intelligence and build up Dad instead?

This is another of hundreds of questions that I can never, ever ask her.

I toss the paper aside and start digging through a stack of notebooks, searching for some clue about who Mom was. Maybe a draft of a letter to John, or a note for a date in a day planner? I pick up a pink notebook with a cracked cover and see written across it in block letters ENGLISH ROMANTIC POETRY, the class where she met Dad. I open it to more scribbled notes. Mom favored blue ink ballpoints, but in the corner of one page is the black ink of a felt tip, the kind Dad likes. It says, in his angular, squarish writing, "Why so glum?" That's all.

Mom and Dad must have been sitting next to each other in class, and Dad wrote a little note to her in her notebook. I imagine him doing it, smiling shyly with his large brown eyes, raising his eyebrows, hopeful. I wish I could know what Mom answered. If she did answer, she probably wrote it in his notebook. I start looking through all the pages, searching for more notes from Dad, when Xander startles the hell out of me.

"What did you just throw away!" She's holding the term paper

I'd tossed aside, her face white with surprise, her dark eyebrows slashed down. "Are you *blind?*"

"What?" I yell.

"Girls, keep your tone civil, please!" Doris says from the corner where she's sunk into a big box full of clothes, half asleep. "You're freaking me out!"

Dramatically, Xander holds up the paper and reads the first page out loud: "Marie Lillian Vogel, Romantic Poetry, five May nineteen eighty, *Professor John Phillips.*"

DARTMOUTH

THE TRIP BACK HOME IS QUIET.

Xander is all red-rimmed and tapped out. She's squeezing her fingers around the steering wheel like she's checking to make sure it's still solid. I think she's even more freaked out than I am. John Phillips taught the Romantic poetry class where Mom and Dad met. All the time she was dating Dad, she was diddling the professor, and lying to Dad about it. She must have been. There's no other explanation.

Doris kept insisting that nothing proves they slept together, but then Xander told her what I wouldn't, that the statue she gave Phillips was worth six thousand dollars, that he'd given it to her in 1995. By the time we left this morning, Doris was as upset as we were.

I thought I knew who my Mom was, but now it's like she's a stranger.

"Hanover is practically on the way, you know."

It's been so long since Xander has spoken, I'm jolted in my seat. My back is killing me. I couldn't sleep at all last night, and I'm sore and exhausted all through my body. "Fine."

I knew she'd want to go to Dartmouth to look for Phillips. Why fight it?

Xander flips the turn signal when we reach the exit to Hanover. I hear a little sniff, and I catch a tear glistening in the corner of her eye. She dabs at it with her thumb.

"It's going to be okay. She's still Mom," I tell her, even though I'm not sure I really believe this anymore. "Besides, your birthday is in a week. You'll probably get another letter."

"I know," she says, her voice scraggly. "I'm just emotional because of all the pot I smoked this weekend."

It's true, she smoked again last night after Doris went to bed. I asked her about it, but she just shrugged like it didn't matter.

"You *should* be crying," I tell Xander. "I don't know why you have to always *know* everything."

"I'm sorry," she says through a voice that sounds slit down the middle. "I shouldn't have started digging into all this. You were right."

My anger shrinks away at this First Ever Admission of Guilt from Xander Vogel. I should record the date and time, because it's not likely to ever happen again. She's so dejected that I want to offer her an olive branch. "We're committed now. There's no use fighting about it."

She chuckles. "You sound like Mom."

We pull in to Hanover, a little New England town a lot like all the others, with handsome old houses and churches with white steeples, only this town has fresh paint over everything, and shiny windows, and well-kept lawns, and lots of pretty people walking pretty dogs. It's easy to see that there's a lot more money here than in our town, but I like our version of New England better, chipped paint and all.

We follow the signs to Dartmouth College. Xander brazenly parks in the faculty parking lot, and we get out and walk across the perfectly manicured lawn to the first big building we find. It looks like a church, made of red brick with a tall white spire, but it turns out to be the library, and just inside the door is a little pamphlet stand. Xander grabs a campus map, and we scan it, looking for the Department of Comparative Literature.

We have to cross the campus, weaving between big buildings that look like huge mansions. Most of them are made of red brick with white trim, but some of them are painted a sparkling white, and their windows seem black by contrast. There are flowers of every size and color planted across campus, though it's summer and there are hardly any students here to enjoy them. A man carrying a large pile of books zooms by us, and Xander turns to watch him go. She isn't so sad anymore. She seems excited, and I realize that soon she's going to be in a place like this.

The thought catches me cold. "Xander! It's Monday! You have to let the universities know today!"

She looks at me blankly. "I called before we left Doris's. You were in the shower."

"Whoa! And you didn't tell me?" I grab her elbow to slow her down. "Well?"

She looks sad, like she doesn't want to tell me, so I know where she chose.

"You're going to *Caltech?*"

She nods, her face mushy like she's going to start crying again.

"*Why?*"

"They have a more theoretical program, and I want to go into research."

"But it's so far away!" Tears slide down my cheeks, and I press my palms against them. The motion makes my back seize up, and I wince.

"Zen, even if I went to Boston, you'd never see me. I'd be working too hard."

"You could come home for long weekends!"

"But I have to do what's right for my future. Caltech is better for me."

"You just want to get away from us so you can turn into a total slut!" I yell at her.

Xander turns away and starts walking again, her feet plodding through the short green grass.

I'm too upset, and in too much pain, to care that Xander feels bad.

We finally get to the hall where the Department of Comparative Literature is, and Xander holds the heavy door open for me. Once we're inside, I realize how hot it is today. The air feels cool on my cheeks, and I take deep breaths to calm myself down. This is turning out to be the second-worst summer of my life. When Mom was dying—that's still number one.

The lobby is dark, and we can see through the little windows in the doors that all the offices are empty. We climb some worn stone stairs up to the second story, where we find only one door open. A plump woman is sitting at a tiny desk, surrounded by what looks like a national disaster involving office supplies. She's humming as she sorts through nametags and fastens them to hundreds of black folders. "Excuse me," Xander says.

"Oh!" the woman cries, startled. "I didn't see you!"

"We're looking for Professor John Phillips?" Xander says in her most confident, professional-sounding voice. Only someone who knows her well would know she's been crying.

The woman crinkles her eyes. "He couldn't be in Comparative Literature."

Xander wilts a little. "Then he must be a former faculty member," she says. "He taught here in the eighties?"

The secretary's eyes wander over the mess in front of her as she thinks. "That was before my time, but I might have something about him in our files." She starts to get up, but seems to think better of it. "Would you mind telling me what this is about?"

Xander stares at her for a second, kind of stunned. I sense something building in the room, and I take a step toward her to stop her, but I'm too late. She totally vomits up the entire story, seeds and all. It goes something like this: "Our mom and dad met here in graduate school . . . she sent off this bird statue . . . we're afraid Mom might have a past with this man . . . we're just looking for some answers."

As she talks my eyes get wider and wider, and finally my mouth drops open. I squeeze her elbow to stop her, but she is like a giant truckload of cow manure cruising downhill with shot brakes.

I look at the plump secretary, trying to gauge her reaction. She's leaning in closer and closer as though gossip is a drug and she's a desperate junkie. Finally Xander sputters to a stop, and the woman just stares for a second, but then she does something I never would have anticipated. She gets up, walks around the desk, and gives Xander a big hug. She pats her back and says, "I'll look through my old files. Just sit tight, hon."

"What the hell was that?" I ask her after the secretary leaves.

She shrugs. "I figured I couldn't come up with a better story than the truth."

We walk over to an ugly, threadbare couch in the corner of the room, and we both sink into it.

It takes a long time, but the secretary finally comes back with a folder in her hand. "I found it!" she says triumphantly. "He was a visiting professor here, fresh from his Ph.D. program at Brandeis. I don't know for sure where he went from here, but I do have a few copies of recommendation letters that were sent out on his behalf. These are the schools." She hands Xander a list of what looks like a dozen schools. "Of course, you didn't get this from me. In fact, we've never met."

"Thank you," Xander whispers. She stands up, gives the secretary another hug, and shuffles me out the door.

Once we get outside, she reads over the list of schools quickly and hands it to me. They're spread all over the country, but if he is still working at one of them, we'll be sure to find him. I get butterflies in my stomach imagining talking to him, and while Xander drives I fall asleep, haunted by restless dreams.

It's almost dusk by the time we get home. The streets are quiet and small in the dim light. A cat trots across the street in front of us. "Make a wish," Xander says out of habit.

I roll my eyes. When I was a kid, for a long time Xander had me believing that when a cat crosses in front of you, you're supposed to make a wish. She also had me looking into the toilet after I went number two for clues about my future, like some people do with tea leaves. I got over that one, but I still sometimes wish on cats.

As we pass by it, I watch the dark feline shape lazily slinking between two cars. *Please let us find out Mom was innocent. That she's who we thought she was.*

The house is dark. Xander turns on the light and we stand in the doorway, looking at our home, not talking. The crystal mantel clock is ticking quietly. Dad's Sunday newspaper is spread out on the coffee table, the book review section on top. That was the only section Mom would ever read. The moonlight glows on the pinewood floor in a ghostly yellow streak that leads toward the staircase. I could almost believe this is a room Mom left just a moment ago. I close my eyes and smell the air for her scent, but all I smell is a garlicky hint of some pizza Dad must have ordered for dinner.

I hear a creak on the basement stairs, and Dad hobbles into the room, arms held out to hug us. We let him, though I can tell by the way Xander's face is all scrunched up that the odor of stale, depressed Dad isn't doing it for her, either.

"How're my girls?" he asks, his voice husky with relief at seeing us.

"We're good," Xander says into his sweatshirt.

"You had a visitor," he tells me as he releases us. "Some kid carrying a camera."

I stare at him blankly before I remember the boy I'd met at the prom. "Oh yeah. For the yearbook committee."

Xander's ears prick up at this, but she says nothing about it, for now.

"How's Doris?" Dad plops backwards into his armchair, letting out an old-man groan.

"A little burned out," Xander says. "A little daffy."

"So, unchanged," he says, nodding approval.

"Speaking of unchanged," she says ominously, "is that the same sweatshirt I saw you wearing when we left? Three days ago?"

"I might have washed it," he says teasingly.

"You might have slept in it," I say. I'm trying to hide my disdain, but I know he can see it on my face, even in the dark room. I'm starting to lose patience with him. We're all sad about Mom, but at least Xander and I haven't given up.

"I know, girls," Dad says, his face long with embarrassment. "I'm beginning to think my sabbatical was perhaps not the wisest choice."

"Have you gotten *anything* done?" I ask him.

He shrugs.

"Don't you have to do *something?*" Xander nags. "An article? Anything? Isn't the department going to expect something to show for all this time off?"

"I'm tenured," he says with a shrug.

Xander tilts her head at him. He drops his eyes to his watch, which has carved a depression in his wrist. I don't think he's taken it off since Mom died. I have a private theory that he's trying to avoid seeing the love poem she'd had engraved on the back of it. "It's late, girls," he says, not because he's tired, but because he doesn't want to talk about how he's not working. "Good night," he says as he shuffles to the basement door.

"Sloth," Xander calls after him.

"Go soak your head in broth," he tells her as he starts down the stairs.

"Take that stinky sweatshirt off!" I yell.

"But I like the feel of the cloth!" he yells back.

"You smell like a horde of goths!" Xander yells louder, never to be outdone at a Vogel rhyme-off.

Dad doesn't answer, so we go into the kitchen for a late snack. Xander turns on the light, which makes us both blink. The kitchen feels fake, like it was taken apart while we were away and reassembled almost right. I want to ask Xander if she feels the same way, but she's looking down the doorway that leads to the basement where Dad has gone, her eyes wide and absent, her expression blank. Suddenly I don't want to ask her what she's thinking about. I want to be alone.

I get a banana and go up to my bedroom. There's a note on my pillow, and I click on my reading lamp.

Dear Goddess of Wisdom,

Your dad thinks I'm stalking you. Sorry.

I lost your phone number because my mom took my leisure suit to the Goodwill in an attempt to rehabilitate my fashion sense. Your number was in the pocket. I was despondent, but I remembered that you are Xander Vogel's sister, and I asked her pizza parlor friend where you lived, and she told me. Now that I think about it, you should probably ask that girl not to go around telling strange guys where you live.

So I came by your house with my camera hoping to get a few frames of you demolishing something, and your dad answered the door, and he seemed very concerned that I tracked you down. So I decided to leave you a note assuring you that I'm not a crazed fiend. In case he says something.

If you're still willing to let me take your picture, please contact me at 245-5984. But please don't give my number to any crazed fiends. Only now am I waking up to the terrible danger of stalkers.

Paul

The last part of the note makes me laugh, and that makes my back hurt, so I lie down on my mattress. It feels unbelievably good to be in my own bed with the feather mattress and flannel sheets, and for a minute I weigh the pros and cons of falling asleep without brushing my teeth.

I'm young. What's a little tartar?

Pretenses

"Are you going to call him?" I don't have to look to know she's waving Paul's note in the air like it's a winning lottery ticket.

I open my eyes to a view of Xander's belly button. At first I think she has lint in it, but then I realize she's had it pierced and there's a garish rhinestone stud in it. "When did you have that done?"

"Last week with Margot. It doesn't hurt if you're drunk."

"That's what you said to the last guy you seduced."

"Funny ha-ha." She flaps Paul's note in my face. "Is he cute?"

I try to remember what he looked like, but all I can picture is that terrible polyester suit. "Not really. I think he had shiny hair." I rub the sleep out of my eyes. I try to move, but my whole back has completely stiffened up.

"Paul Martelli. He's Italian." She gently sits down on my mattress instead of just plopping down and bouncing the way she usually does. She must be able to tell that I'm in pain. "Swarthy can be good."

"He wasn't swarthy so much as . . . I don't know. Goofy."

"Goofy can be good." She scans his note again. "Yeah, he's funny. I like him."

"Go out with him then."

"He's hitting on *you,* dumbass." She gets up and goes into the bathroom. For a second I think I might be in the clear, but then she comes back with a Motrin and a cup of water. "Take."

"He just wants my picture for the yearbook," I say before knocking back the drugs. "It's not like he's hitting on me."

"Come on. You're not that stupid."

I close my eyes like I'm falling back asleep.

She's right, I'm not that stupid. I just don't want her input on anything to do with Paul Martelli. For weeks now, ever since I went to the prom with Adam, she's been itching for me to start dating and get laid, and she'll stop at nothing short of actually putting the condom on the guy herself. The less she knows about Paul the better. "He's ugly," I finally have the presence of mind to say.

"Nice try. What are you going to wear?" She opens up my closet and starts pawing at my clothes. "Jesus, Zen, don't you own anything that isn't Puritan?"

"Don't knock the Puritans. They had nice belt buckles."

"Everything is gray and brown! You need red."

"He's taking a picture of me doing shotokan. I'll be wearing my gi."

"Ugh. Those stupid pajama pants give you grandmother-ass."

"Too bad."

"I have the perfect top for you. And you should let me do your hair." She sits down next to me again and smoothes my hair out of my eyes. This is something Mom used to do. I think Xander realizes she just reminded me of Mom, because she pulls back a little, her mouth twisting in a pout. "Anyway, Zen, this is good. You should go out with him. See if you like him." She stares out the window, a weird, determined look on her face.

I can't see where she's looking without wrenching my back, but if I had to guess, I'd say she's looking at Adam's house. "Why don't you just tell him how you feel?"

"Who?" she asks innocently. She doesn't look at me, but at the floor, as though this conversation isn't worth the effort to lift her eyes.

I just stare at her and wait. This is the only way to cut through her crap.

She sighs angrily. "I'm a slut, Zen, remember? I don't date guys I care about."

"Why not?"

"I just want to have fun." Her face takes on a hard expression.

"Fine," I tell her. "Thanks for the Motrin."

She walks out of my room and I try to drift to sleep, but I hear her march back in and drop something heavy onto my bed. I open my eyes to discover a phone in my face. "Call him, then sleep," she says, arms folded.

"Bossy," I growl. "Leave the room."

She backs out and closes the door, but I know she's standing just outside listening because I can see her shadow under the door.

I dial Paul's number, my mind racing, as if choosing the right greeting will assure the survival of the human race. *Hello? Hey? Hiya? Good morning? What's happening?* The phone clicks on the other end, and I hear a guy's voice, much deeper than I remember from the prom. "Hello, goddess."

Damn it. Caller ID. "Hi, stalker."

"I was afraid my leisure suit might have frightened you off."

"I'm a brave woman."

"So, when can I come over and watch you bust some boards?"

"I'm not in board-busting shape at the moment. I threw out my back."

"Ouch. You okay?"

"I just need to take it easy."

"Need a male nurse?"

I'm not sure what to say. Is he suggesting a sponge bath? Or just being funny? Suddenly I feel awkward. "Um . . ."

"Well, I'm not one. No medical training whatsoever, actually. But I could photo-document your misery."

"If you must."

"How about you just put on your white outfit and stand there with your fists raised?"

"That I can do. Probably in a few days."

"Okay, how about Wednesday then? At like eleven?"

"Sounds fine. Just come by."

"Um, your father doesn't own a gun, does he?"

"Just don't make any sudden moves."

As I hang up, I realize that my fingers are white and shaking. I liked the way his voice sounded, deep and throaty, but clear too. And he's smart. I can tell by the rhythm of his speech.

Xander bursts through the door. "That was good! You sounded cool. You only said one really funny thing, but I think it's better to be dull than to try too hard to be funny, because then you just come off as desperate."

"Thanks for the critique."

"Least I can do." She holds up a red shirt and wiggles it at me. "This will go great with your tits."

"I'm wearing my gi!"

"For the photo shoot. For the date, you'll wear this shirt and those nice jeans I got you for Christmas that you never wear."

"Because *you're* always wearing them."

"I know how to appreciate a fine garment. They'll make your ass into a tight little cream puff for our Paulie," she says as she backs out of my room, a wicked smile on her face.

Why did I think I could keep her out of this? She's like radioactive gas. She leaks in through the tiny cracks in the walls and fills up the entire room.

She grants me a grand total of thirty peaceful minutes before she comes in again, papers in her hand. "He's at Marquette!" she yells. She's holding a jar of Vicks VapoRub.

"What's that for?"

"Turn over. I'll rub." She slaps at my thigh until I turn, and bends over me. "Tell me how hard."

I feel the horrible coldness of Vicks on my back, but as it melts into my skin, my tight muscles dissolve. Xander gently rubs her palm over my back, up and down, until I can release my tension enough so that she can really knead. It hurts, but it feels nice, too. "You can push harder," I tell her.

"That's what you'll be telling Paul this weekend."

"Gross, Xander."

"So Phillips is at Marquette. That's in Wisconsin. Where they have cheese." She works a knuckle into a hollow near my spine until I wriggle. "And football."

"Did you get his phone number?"

"I think we should go there. People are more forthcoming in person."

"Have fun."

"Like I'd ever *let* you stay home."

"Xander, where will we get the money for a trip like that? It's not like we can ask Dad for it."

She's silent as she works her fingers into a knot between my shoulder blades. For a second it hurts so much that I want to tell her to stop, but then it starts to loosen up, and I find I can take it. "We'll let your back heal up a little before we go."

"Gee, thanks. In the meantime I'll build us a flying machine to get us there."

"I'll figure out that stuff."

"I think we should try calling the guy, first," I say.

"That's why I'm the one who does all the thinking."

Xander plunges her fingers into my lower back, and for a while I'm incapable of speech. I turn my head toward my dresser and see the red shirt Xander wants me to wear draped over my mirror. It's a sexy little V-neck, with tiny pearl buttons down the front. It looks soft and comfortable, and not too showoffy. It's pretty.

She's probably right. It would look great on me.

But I'm not going to Wisconsin.

PAUL

THE DOORBELL RINGS, and I slowly pull myself upright and walk to the door. My heart feels like it's wiggling around in my ribs, but I don't know why I'm nervous. I'm not even really attracted to Paul. At least, I wasn't at the prom.

I open the door, and he's standing in front of me with a crooked smile, holding an enormous camera. He takes in my gi, and my bare feet, and he presses his palms together and bows deeply, just like they do in Bruce Lee movies.

"Konnichiwa," he says.

"Huh?" I retort.

"Japanese for 'good afternoon.' I don't know the word for 'morning.'"

"Oh. Um. *Konnichiwa* to you, too." I open the door wide for him and he sort of slides in sideways, like he's nervous my dad is going to leap out at him from behind the sofa.

"Dad's taking a nap," I say, trying to make that statement sound normal at eleven in the morning. "He's really tired lately," I add, as if that explains anything.

"Oh, okay." He shrugs.

"Iced tea?" I ask him. Xander forced me to make a pitcher ahead of time, insisting you should have something besides water and fermented apple juice to offer a guy. Now I'm kind of glad that she did, because it gives me something to say. I'm even more nervous now that he's here, because I realize that it was the leisure suit that made him look ugly. His hair is shiny, his eyes a pretty hazel color, his skin perfectly even and tan, and he's tall. Taller than Adam. Taller than Dad. I like tall. "It's brewed, not instant," I add, like any teenage guy would care about that.

"Oh, lovely," he says, and winces at his use of a girly word. "I mean, okay."

I lead him back to the kitchen, which looks pretty clean except for the floor, which is sticky on the soles of my feet. I have to lift the iced tea pitcher with both hands because it's heavy and my back can't take the weight. I pour two glasses and hand one to Paul.

"*Domo arigato,*" he says before raising it to his lips.

"*De nada.*"

He chuckles, and that helps some of my nervousness fade away. As he drinks his tea, I look at him more closely. He's wearing a white T-shirt with a picture of Gumby on it, and plain blue jeans. Not the expensive kind, but regular Levi's, which I like. Guys who spend a lot of money on clothes are kind of a turnoff for me. He's wearing the same Birkenstocks that he'd worn to the prom, and in the daylight I can see how broken down they are. I bet they're his only pair of shoes. Or the only ones he wears, anyway.

"Where should we do this?" he asks me as he wipes tea off his chin.

"Backyard?"

He looks out the kitchen window and nods. "Good light."

For a while, it's all business. I hold up my fists, and I can even balance well enough to do a very slow side kick. Soon, though, I have to sit down to rest my back, and he takes a seat next to me on the bench in the gazebo.

"Who's the bird freak?" he asks me, his eyes on the dozen bird feeders hanging in the trees behind our house. With a pang I realize they're all empty. Mom was the one who always bought the birdseed.

"My mom was," I say.

"*Was?*"

I look at his twitching mouth. "She died last year," I say.

He's quiet as he takes this in.

"I thought everyone knew."

"Why would everyone know?"

"You know how bad news travels." I watch as a raven circles over our house, high above. Or maybe it's a crow. Mom would know the difference. "People talk."

"Well, I'm sorry to hear about that."

"Oh, that's okay," I say. "She was kind of a pain in the ass." I wait to see what he does.

He narrows his eyes at me, kind of amused, but mostly just thinking. "Really?"

Something about the way he's half smiling makes my jauntiness take a dive. "No. I just don't like people feeling sorry for me."

"Okay." He's looking at me with too much intensity, and I want to move away from him. I need to.

"I'm hungry," I say as I stand up.

"I know a place that makes great french fries." He screws his lens cap on carefully, as though the camera is a beloved, delicate pet.

"I'll go get changed." I turn my back on him. Even though he's cute, and nice, and funny, I want to get away because he makes me feel too jumpy.

I go up to my room and change into my date clothes. The jeans Xander wants me to wear are a little too tight for my taste, but I do wear the red shirt, which makes my skin look bronzed and sexy. I slip into my loose Levi jeans and dig through my closet until I find my most comfortable loafers. I pull my hair out of its ponytail and brush it until it's shiny and smooth. That's the only good thing about having fine hair—it's glossy.

When I come back downstairs, Paul's eyes travel up and down my body, and I suddenly wish I'd worn a regular T-shirt. Am I sending the wrong signals? What signals do I want to send?

Paul drives us in his little yellow car. It's an ancient Beetle with rust crawling all over the doors, but it feels like a tank as we buzz down the street. It doesn't have air conditioning, so we roll down the windows. The engine is so loud that we don't talk, but I find myself smiling the whole way. His car is a junker, but it's fun.

We park outside the french fries place and a woman comes out to our car to take our order. Our town still has a lot of old-fashioned places like this. Drive-in movies, antique soda fountains, trolley cars, and even an old steam engine train that still runs. Al's French Fries, a real drive-in diner, is my favorite. When the waitress comes out with our root beer floats and fries, and I smell the salty grease and taste the sweet creamy soda, I'm glad I live here, where people know how to hold on to the good parts of the past.

"What year are you?" I ask Paul, just for something to talk about.

"I'm a senior next year. Same as you."

"Are you planning on going to college?"

"Oh, yeah. For sure."

"What do you want to study?"

He stuffs a few fries into his mouth, looking at me wryly. "Most people regret asking me that."

"I think I can take it."

"Okay. I want to study theology."

"Theology? You mean about God?"

"Yeah. And religion." He says this defiantly, like he expects me to make fun of him.

"Do you want to be a priest or something?" I ask, suddenly very disappointed. I hadn't even noticed that somewhere along the line, I'd started to like him. As in *like* like.

"God, no," he says, then seems to hear himself and chuckles. "No. I'm just interested in the phenomenon of religion." He looks through the windshield at the trees swaying in the wind. Right behind Al's is a small stream, with tons of trees and bushes crowded around it to drink. I can hear the gurgle of the water through our open car windows, and it sounds just like a lullaby to me. I glance again at Paul, who seems to be thinking hard as he looks at the millions of green leaves. Something he's thinking about seems to get him excited, and he turns to me, animated. "Did you know that every human culture has some form of religion?"

"I've never really thought about it."

"So either," he says, jabbing a french fry into the air for emphasis, "either there's an innate human need for some belief structure, or there really is a creator that we kind of sense somewhere up there, in the ether."

Xander would be throwing a conniption. She thinks that religion amounts to a fairy tale for children that people make up because they don't want to believe they can really die. "So I guess you're pretty religious, huh?" I try to keep the judgment out of my voice.

"Not really. My family is Unitarian, but we don't go to church every weekend. I just find religion fascinating."

So he's not a fanatic, but still, something about this conversation makes my hackles rise.

We eat our fries and sip our floats for a minute. I snatch little glances at him, watching his square jaw work at his food, his hazel eyes dance around. He's not talking, but he's thinking. I have a feeling he's always thinking. "But you must believe in God," I finally say.

He thinks about this for a second, and I wait patiently. I don't mind this about him, because I'm the same way. When someone asks me a big question, I have to take some time to think. Not everyone can stand the wait.

Finally, he puts his float down on the tray between us. "Yeah, I do believe in God. I'm not sure what He—excuse me—*She* looks like, or is like, but somehow the universe seems to make more sense if there's a . . . I don't know, a *cause* behind everything. You know? Evolution explains *how* we came to be. But nothing really explains *why.* And that's the question I want to study—why?"

"You'll never get an answer."

"I know." He beams me with a brilliant smile. "What about you? Do you believe in God?"

It seems to make him happy to be talking about this with me. It doesn't make me happy, though.

I lean my head back while I think about it. Dad quotes literature the way some people quote the Bible, and that always felt like enough for me. But when Mom died, I wondered where she went. An entire person, all her thoughts, her feelings, her personality, her sense of humor, her laugh, her *being*—could all of that really *vanish?* Somehow my mind can't accept that. Xander would say believing in the afterlife is wishful thinking, but I'm not sure it is. I believe, or maybe I just hope, that there's an afterlife of some kind.

And what about that voice I hear in my mind? That's real, isn't it? I want it to be, anyway.

Whether there's a god making all the decisions, though, I'm not sure. If there is a god, he's not the kind, loving grandfather a lot of people claim he is. If he were, I'd still have a mother. And people wouldn't be allowed to die the way Mom died, in terrible pain, and hunger, and thirst, with no hope of relief except the end. The end of everything.

I remember that Paul is still waiting for an answer, a slight smile on his lips as he looks at me. I clear my throat. "I think I believe that maybe a person's soul goes somewhere after they die, but I guess I don't really believe in God."

He squints at me, bemused. "No one has ever told me that."

"What?"

"That they believe in an afterlife, but not in God."

I shrug. "It's just, I think if there was really some perfect being who could fix things, the world wouldn't be so miserable, you know?"

"I know what you mean. If God is supposed to be such a great guy, why do little children starve to death?"

I nod.

Most of the time when I tell believers I don't believe, they get angry, or defensive. But Paul doesn't. He chews on his straw for a while as he thinks about it. Chewing isn't quite the right word. He grabs it in his teeth and pulls on it really hard, as though he's trying to stretch it. Once he knows what he wants to say, he pulls the mangled straw out of his mouth. "I guess I think of God like my fifth grade substitute teacher snogging the principal of my school."

"Okay," I say, in all seriousness, "that's weird, Paul."

He laughs. "No! I'll explain. When I was in fifth grade, we had this substitute, Mrs. Evans, filling in for our regular teacher who was having some kind of surgery. Mrs. Evans was tall, like at least six feet, and kind of big. Not fat, I guess, just a large, beefy woman. She had superlong hair that hung past her butt, and she had the kind of nose where you can sort of see inside her nostrils. Anyway it came out later that year that she'd been schtooping the principal. I guess the school secretary caught them necking in his office one day. She was a total gossip, and she told a few mothers, and before you knew it the entire school was abuzz about it. Mrs. Evans and Mr. Sloate acted really embarrassed too. They'd slink around the hallways while all the kids whispered about them."

"And this has to do with God because . . ."

He shakes his head, like there's a train inside it and he's trying to bounce it onto the right track. "Um. Incomprehensibility. I could not imagine, could not begin to wrap my mind around the fact that they'd ever touched each other, because she was so big, and he was so . . . He was bald. I didn't tell you that part. Bald, and he always had bloodshot eyes. To me, they were both so old and ugly! Anyway,

I finally asked my mom how two such ugly people could find each other attractive enough to do *that*." He wrinkles his nose in mock disgust. "Mom just said, 'You know, Paul, all I can say is it's a grownup thing.'" He stops, looking out the windshield at all the fluffy trees, quietly nodding to himself.

"I'm still not getting the connection."

He gives me a sly grin, and that makes me smile. Somewhere along the way, my hackles went down. I like this Paul Martelli. I really do.

"Last year I saw Mrs. Evans in the supermarket," he says, his voice low. "I didn't talk to her or anything, but I did get a good look at her. Now that I'm older, I can see she's kind of a pretty woman. I'm not a kid anymore. I went up a level, and now I understand someone wanting to snog her. Know what I mean?"

"Kind of," I say, because I don't want him to think I'm a moron. I'm trying to follow what he's saying, but I'm a little distracted by a small chip in his front tooth, which is amazingly sexy in a way I cannot describe.

"It's like God is a grownup and we're all fifth-graders," he says. He sees the new way I'm looking at him, and now he's looking at me in that way too, and his voice is softer, as though it's being slowly caressed by his breath. "The bad stuff He lets happen, to Him it's a grownup thing." He fixes me with a level gaze. "Just like I couldn't imagine Mr. Sloate's reasons for wanting to do the nasty with Mrs. Evans, I can't understand God's reasons either."

We look at each other for a long time, slowly smiling.

The Phone Call

"Either he's really deep, or he's really weird," Xander says. I'm lying on the living room couch, she's perched on the armrest, and we're dissecting my date. At least, she is. "So he didn't even *act* like he wanted to kiss you?"

"I don't *know* if he wanted to kiss me, Xander. I'm not a mind reader."

"There are signals."

I get so sick of her explaining guys to me, as if they are that complicated. Either they like you or they don't. It's not like Paul is a sports car I have to hot-wire.

"Did he look at your lips a lot? Did he lean in? Did he—"

"Oh, spare me!"

"But he *did* drive you home?"

"No, Xander, he kicked me out of his car and made me walk four miles with a sore back."

"Wow. What a jerk," she says, just to get on my nerves.

"He said let's do this again. So maybe he'll kiss me later."

"Or maybe he just wants to be friends."

Xander can't handle ambiguity, and I guess if my afternoon with Paul was anything, it was ambiguous. We talked for hours about God, religion, our futures, and then he drove me home. It felt friendly in the car, and breezy. I didn't feel all knotted up the way I usually am when I'm around a guy I think is cute, maybe because I could see the side of Paul that doesn't depend on him being attractive. He parked under the big maple tree that shades our lawn. He said, "Let's do this again." Then, the feel of his fingertip on my skin, and I got out of the car.

"Well—" I begin. But then I think better of it. I shouldn't tell Xander anything.

"Well what?"

I sigh. Judging from the way she's sitting, with her elbows on her knees, leaning forward, staring avidly into my face, there's no way she's going to drop this. I may as well give her what she wants, and what she wants is details. "I guess I didn't give him a chance to kiss me because I got out of the car pretty fast."

She throws up her hands. "God! Zen! You need girl lessons, I swear to god!"

"But before I got out," I yell so she'll shut up, "he touched my arm. Very lightly. Sort of in the crease of my elbow. With one finger."

She stares at me, deadpan "That's so sexy I'm about to climax right here."

"Shut up. It was nice." He waited for me to open the front door before he drove off. I liked that, though I know Xander would see this as unimportant. To me, it's very important. Every guy wants to touch, but not every guy waits to make sure you get in okay. "He wasn't grabby. So what?"

This seems to satisfy her. "Okay. Good. You're on track."

"On track for *what?*"

"On track for no longer being a hopelessly virginal martial arts geek."

"Like being a slutty martial arts geek is something to shoot for."

"You'd be better off, believe me."

"Whatever."

She slaps her hands together and rubs them like she's at a hoedown and the roast pig is ready. "Okay. You wanted to call what's-his-bucket. So let's do it."

Even though I'm lying down, this makes my stomach plunge. "I thought you wanted to go there without calling."

"I checked in to plane fare, and I can't find any tickets for less than six hundred dollars." She picks up the phone from the end table behind her. "Come on. Let's just do it."

"It's too late to call right now."

"Not in Wisconsin."

"I don't want to do it."

"Okay. I will." She cradles the phone on her shoulder and punches the keys, but just as quickly hangs back up. "I can't." She starts chewing on the corner of her fingernail absently, a signal she's thinking extra hard. She narrows her eyes at the window. "We need a man."

"That's what you said last week when you and Margot were making out."

"Ha-ha." She sticks the phone in my face. "Call Adam."

"What the hell for?"

"Adam can pretend to be Mr. Blackstone following up about Mom's will. About the statue."

"Call him yourself. I'm not going to be your go-between."

She glares at me like she wants to belt me as she eases into the red armchair that Mom used to always sit in. The room is dark, but there's lots of light filtering through the thin curtains. She's sitting so still, thinking, blue in the moonlight, if I blur my eyes enough, I can almost believe Xander is Mom, like I'm looking at a ghost. And the ghost is terribly sad.

Xander breaks the spell when she clicks on the table lamp at my feet, lifts the phone, and dials Adam's number. "Hey. It's me . . . *Xander*, you asshole. We need your help . . . Well, Zen needs your help . . . Apologize for what? . . . *I'm* giving *you* the silent treatment? . . . Fine, Adam, I'm sorry you have the emotional maturity of a zygote. Can you *please* come help us? Now? . . . Fine. Bye." She jabs at the phone to turn it off, and throws it into the easy chair across the living room. It bounces onto the floor with a loud crack.

"Hey! If you're going to throw things, go outside!" Dad calls up from the bowels of the basement.

"I'm glad to hear you haven't died!" Xander calls back.

"No, I'm just lying here on my side!" Dad calls back.

"I'm starting to think you have no pride!" I yell.

"I know," he calls. It worries me that he didn't rhyme. I should go down to check on him, but I don't have the energy. Dad is going to have to find his own way out of the basement.

Xander goes upstairs and into the bathroom. I hear her splashing water on her face, opening and closing makeup containers. She's getting ready for Adam, though she'd never admit it, probably not even to herself.

Adam knocks as he opens the front door and steps inside. He's wearing jeans and a button-down shirt. When he sees Xander coming downstairs, he skips a beat before saying, "Hi."

"Hi," we both drone.

Xander hands him the phone. "I need you to pretend to be Mr. Blackstone, Mom's lawyer, and you're calling Phillips to check that the statue arrived safely. Or something."

"Or something?"

"Just do it," she snaps. "You're good with people. Milk him for information."

"About what?"

"Find out if he had an affair with Mom," she whispers so Dad can't hear, "but don't *seem* like you're trying to find it out." She hands him the paper with Phillips's number on it and plunks onto the sofa, barely giving me enough time to move my feet out of the way.

She could get the phone from upstairs and listen to the whole conversation, but she doesn't, and that's not like Xander. I realize now that the real reason she got Adam is because she's scared, just like I am. I don't even want to hear the guy's voice.

"Don't say anything stupid," Xander says.

"And don't ask him outright," I add.

"Make it sound like a business call."

"Shut up!" Adam shakes his head angrily as he dials, but when the other end clicks on, he's all professional courtesy. "Hello, is this Mr. Phillips?—Doctor. Sorry. I'm sorry to bother you at home. This is uh, uh . . ." He widens his eyes in horror and looks at Xander, who mouths the word at him. "Bob Blackstone, and I'm calling regarding Marie Vogel's will? . . . Well, I'm glad we could be of service. . . . Dr. Phillips, I've gotten an inquiry from the family about the statue I sent you. It was one of the oldest daughter's favorites. It would help her to understand why her mother left you the statue if she knew the nature of your relationship?"

Xander gives Adam a thumbs-up.

Adam pauses for a long time, listening. I search his face for some clue about what Phillips is saying, but he's completely blank. Finally he nods. "I see. So it was purely professional? Because the family has learned the value of the statue and—" Adam winces, and I can hear Phillips's voice coming through the phone in sharp tones. He's mad. "I'm sorry, sir, I didn't realize this was such a delicate subject for you," Adam says innocently, and then Phillips *really* lets him have it. At one point the yelling is so bad, Adam has to hold the phone away from his ear, and I catch a few words.

"Don't you know what this could do to that family!"

I look at Xander, who looks at me, her face grave.

"Sir! Sir! You're right. You're absolutely right. I have no idea how they found out about it, but I promise you I will do everything I can to—" Adam cuts off, surprised, then clicks the phone off. "He hung up."

"What did he say?" Xander asks.

"He said she was his student, but when I started pressing him he got really defensive." His voice is soft as he talks to her, and he's looking at her with very sad eyes.

"You're holding something back," I say to him. His eyes dart to mine, then down to the floor.

"What did he *say?*" Xander asks again.

"When I mentioned you," Adam says slowly, tapping his fingertips nervously on his thigh, "the first thing out of his mouth was 'Her daughters weren't supposed to know about us.'"

"Us," Xander repeats, her eyes on mine.

Mom was lying. To us. To Dad, and to me and Xander. She lied. Not just little lies, either. Huge, guilty, black-as-night lies. About who she was, about her life, about everything.

"There's no dignity in lying" is what she always said to us, with such conviction, her pointy chin jutted out, her eyes fierce. And I knew she was right. As much trouble as Xander and I caused, we never did lie to her. When we were caught, we told the truth and faced the consequences.

Could this really be? Could Mom really have been such a liar? Such a hypocrite? How could she leave behind such a mess? How could she do this to us?

XANDER'S BIRTHDAY

"HAPPY BIRTHDAY, JAYBIRD!" Dad says as he emerges from the basement on the morning of Xander's eighteenth.

"Thanks, Dad," Xander says, bleary-eyed. She's still wearing her clothes from the night before, and she's huddled over her bowl of cereal, taking huge, rueful bites.

Dad lowers himself onto a kitchen chair across from us, rubbing his belly.

"Nice to see you upright," I tell him.

"It's nice to see you at all," Xander adds.

Of course we've seen him around the house, but only in passing, near the kitchen or bathroom. Now that he's sitting at the breakfast table, I can get a good look at him. His blond hair is matted to his head and super greasy. He's grown a beard, and the wiry white hairs are poking out of his cheeks and chin like scraggly blades of grass. His breath smells like he's been subsisting on a diet of roadkill.

But hey, he's up before noon for the first time in months.

Looking at Dad now, sitting here at breakfast, I hurt for him. Does he know that Mom had been with another man?

"Want to go to the Red Lantern tonight?" he asks Xander. "Or we could take in a movie."

"Nah, Dad, thanks," Xander says. She pours milk into her bowl of cereal. "I'm going out with Margot."

"But it's your birthday!" I say. "We're always together on our birthdays!"

She forces a huge bite of Cheerios into her mouth and chews loudly.

"It's your eighteenth. It's special," Dad pleads.

"Let's just get a cake, okay?" I say. "Chocolate? And you can eat it before you go out?"

She picks up her bowl and gets up from the table. "Look, I don't feel like celebrating, okay?"

"Oh, come on!" I whine.

"I mean it!" she yells as she backs out the kitchen door.

Dad and I listen to her pounding up the stairs to her room. Then Dad turns to me. "She leaves us no choice."

I look at him. He's shapeless and smelly and unshaven as ever, but there's a fun little smirk on his face that I haven't seen since before Mom got sick. Dad's mischievous streak is waking up. In fact, it seems like the whole of Dad is waking up from a long hibernation. His shoulders aren't so slouched, his eyes aren't so hooded. He seems ready to stop being a slug, and it's about time. So even though I didn't plan on spending the day arranging Xander's birthday, I latch on to Dad's new mood and suggest, "Surprise party?"

"I'll order the cake. Be quiet about it. She's hard to fool."

The phone call to Phillips has been getting to both of us, but Xander is especially tormented. The fact that Mom probably cheated on Dad, cheated on *us,* is more than Xander can stand. It's easier for me, probably because of my shotokan training. In Buddhism, you learn to accept everything in life without judging it. That's what I've been concentrating on, accepting that Mom had a private life, that she wanted to keep it private, and that John Phillips was a part of that life. It takes a lot of concentration to keep myself from thinking the worst of her. Still, all the meditation in the world won't keep me from feeling angry.

Dad stands up from the table, patting at his belly. "It's time I got off my duff. I think I'll go to the library."

"Shower first."

"Nah!" He winks. "I'll cut through the stockyard to cover my body odor."

"Great idea. While you're at it, swing by the sewer for some mouthwash."

He throws his head back and really laughs at that one. He seems almost happy, like he's been away from me and Xander for a long time and he's glad to be back.

Since Xander has the ears of a bat and the eyes of an eagle, the only way to plan this thing is to use Adam's phone across the street. I slip into my chunky jeans and my Yosemite T-shirt and kick over to his house in my flip-flops. As I cross the street, I look down toward Lake Champlain, which you can see if you crane your neck. The water is brilliant blue and winking in the sunlight, and it makes me feel happy for a second. Things have been bad. They've been really bad, but that doesn't mean life isn't good. It seems like Dad is starting to remember that.

I knock and open the front door. "Hello! Anybody home?"

Nancy bounds out of the kitchen. She's still wearing her red flannel bathrobe that Mom bought for her one Christmas. Her bouncy brown hair is ratted around her small face, and she doesn't have any makeup on, so she looks kind of pale, but really cute too. When I look at Nancy, I never notice her funny features so much as her awesome personality. I can't help but see her as pretty, even though traditionally she's not. "Heya!" she says. "What's the good news?"

"It's Xander's birthday today. We're throwing a surprise party."

"Yippie!" she says and swoops me into a waltz. She whizzes me around the living room, humming Strauss under her breath, her brown eyes looking dreamily on the ceiling. Nancy is a nut.

She twirls onto the soft, poofy couch. I lower myself carefully, feeling at my back to make sure I'm okay. "Oh, damn!" She covers her mouth with her fingers. "I forgot. Did I hurt you?"

"Nah," I say. "Not that fragile."

She jams her shoulder into the couch so she can face me. "How's my odd little neighbor today?"

"Fine. How's my neighborly oddity?"

"Equally fine. Eggs? Coffee?"

"Son?"

"Upstairs."

I go up, calling out in a booming voice, "Adam Little, you're wanted for questioning in connection with being a fuddy-duddy and a general stick in the mud!"

"Not to mention he didn't eat his squash last night at dinner!" Nancy calls.

Adam cracks his door open and I see one bloodshot eye peering into the hallway. "It's eight o'clock in the morning," he intones.

"Time for your enema," I say, tapping my wrist as if I had a watch.

He stares at me blearily for a second, letting me wonder if he's mad at me for waking him up, but then he grins. "Enema before breakfast? How droll!" he says. "Give me a second." And he disappears behind his door again.

I lower myself onto the top step and wait while he gets dressed. The carpet on the stairs is threadbare green, but it looks pretty with the sun shining through the small stained-glass window at the top of the stairs. Squares of yellow and orange light glow on my skin, and I wiggle my fingers, watching them change color. I hear a door click behind me, and a clearing of the throat. Adam is standing on the top step in oversize khaki shorts and a lopsided polo shirt. "Ahem. What are you doing?"

"Tripping on Motrin. Want to help me put together a birthday party for Xander?"

"She *wants* me to help?" he asks, surprised.

"No. She doesn't even want the party." I smile sweetly.

"So this will piss her off and generally make her miserable?"

"That's the overall goal."

"Well then, definitely, yes, I'd like to help." He rubs his hands together and cackles like a mad scientist. "Mwah ha ha ha ha!"

THE PARTY

IT STARTED OUT SMALL and simple. Me, Dad, Adam, Nancy, Margot, and Xander. But then Dad wanted to invite Grandma, and she wanted to bring a friend, which is odd because I didn't realize she *had* friends. Then when Adam and I went to see Margot at the pizzeria, she said her boyfriend would bring his friend along as a blind date for Xander. "He'll be our gift to her!" Margot said, with a satisfied look at Adam's wan face. And then she *had* to say in front of Adam: "Aren't you going to bring that guy, Zen? What's his name?"

At which Adam raised his eyebrows and asked, "Is this a hubba-hubba situation?"

"His name's Paul. And I don't really know what constitutes a hubba-hubba situation." I felt myself turning purple, and at first I didn't want to invite Paul, but then I thought, *Why not? What's stopping me?* So I used Adam's cell phone to get Paul's number from directory assistance, and talked to him right there while Margot served us each a free slice with red pepper flakes and Parmesan.

"I can't go," Paul said, "unless I can bring my cousin along? Would that be okay? She's cute."

What could I say? "Sure, bring her!" Once I hung up I said to Adam, "I think Paul is bringing a blind date for you too. His cousin. He says she's cute."

Adam slapped his forehead. "So how many are we up to?"

Margot counted under her garlicky breath. "Like a dozen?"

"We can't sneak that many people into the living room while Xander's upstairs," I said.

"Let's have it at my house, then," Adam said before taking a disturbingly large bite out of his pizza. Why do guys eat like that?

So we raced back to his house to find Nancy gathering up a box of party decorations. "We're having the party here, Mom," Adam said.

"Not without a good scrubbing," she replied.

So Adam and I spent the whole day vacuuming and dusting and sweeping and mopping, and throwing away old magazines, and organizing his CD collection. Nancy flitted here and there, hanging up streamers and making a huge banner for Xander that said WELCOME TO THE LEGAL VOTING AGE, and blowing up balloons. Dad came in looking freshly shaved, holding a huge sheet cake with sloppy lettering on it that said HAPPY BIRTHDAY, JAYBIRD, and we all sampled a fingerful of white frosting. It was fluffy and too sweet, just like birthday frosting should be.

Margot was supposed to swing by our house at six o'clock and make some excuse to drag Xander over to Adam's, so at five-thirty we called up the Red Lantern, Xander's favorite Chinese restaurant, and we ordered enough General Tso's chicken and Szechuan beef and vegetable lo mein to feed an entire platoon of ninjas. Grandma agreed to pick it up on her way over, under strict instructions from Dad to park in the alley behind Nancy's house and come in the back door so Xander wouldn't see her.

Which is what she does, at five forty-five, to find me, Dad, Nancy, and Adam all leaning on the center island, talking.

"Hello!" she calls in her prissy-polite voice she uses in front of nonfamily. "We come bearing fortune cookies!" She marches in playfully, which is weird because she never does anything that is playful.

Behind her is a man with lots of thick white hair, and a huge smile on his face. His blue eyes follow Grandma's every move. She wipes her feet on Nancy's welcome mat, and he does too. She puts her bags of food on the counter, so he puts his there. When she starts to take off her pressed navy blazer, he jumps into action and takes it from her, looking for a place to hang it.

"This is Neil," she says casually to my father, who is staring at the scene with his mouth fully open.

"Put 'er there, pal!" Neil booms, and shakes Dad's hand hard enough to break a small bone in his wrist. "Neil Ackerson. Do you know Ackerson Muffler and Lube? That's me."

"Oh, yeah, I bought some tires there once." Dad's eyes slide over him in utter confusion. "Pleased to meet you."

"Any son of Felicia's is a friend of mine," he says loudly, and slams Dad in the back a couple times with his palm. It's meant to be a friendly gesture, but it makes Dad shrink away from him. The guy is old, but he's strong.

"Nice to, uh . . ." Dad says, and trails off, staring at his mother.

"Well," Grandma declares, "I'm here, though I didn't get so much as a phone call since Xander's graduation."

"Oh, I'm sorry, Mom," Dad says. "We've just been . . ." He doesn't finish his sentence, probably because he's starting to realize that it's getting a little old, him always playing the grief card.

Grandma's narrow eyes wander the kitchen, over Nancy, who is giggling with Adam, over the cake, which looks even sloppier now that Grandma is looking at it, over the streamers that messily hang over the doorway, finally to my big turquoise earrings, which represent the sum total of effort I put into my appearance tonight, and she sniffs. Sniffing is Grandma's way of expressing displeasure. Then, mechanically, she lifts her arms in a hugging gesture, and nods at me as though I've been standing here longing to hug her and only waiting for permission to run into her arms.

"Hi, Grandma," I say, and pat her back, much more gently than Neil patted Dad. The contact forces a small amount of gas to escape from her ass in a musical little note. "How are you?"

"I'm fine, as you can see," she says coolly. She fluffs the silk scarf at her neck, and Neil leans in to fluff it a little more for her before sliding an arm around her bony back.

"She's as fine as a spring day!" he booms before kissing her forehead, holding his lips to her wrinkled skin for an uncomfortable amount of time. She pats at the side of his head, laughing, a little coy, a little embarrassed. She farts again, this time loudly, but this goes unnoticed by Neil. I realize he probably talks so loud because he's hard of hearing.

If he has a weakened sense of smell, it's a match made in heaven.

Dad watches Grandma cuddling with her date, his face taking on a strange pallor. I imagine that he wishes he could slink back into our basement and hide there until either Neil or Grandma goes into a nursing home. I might join him.

There's a knock on the back kitchen door, and it opens again. In walks Paul, and on his hip is a baby girl who looks about eighteen months old. Curly blond hair floats over her cherub pink face. Grandma sees her and squeals, "Oh! Who's the little lover?"

She holds out her hands and the little girl bounces herself in Paul's arms until he hands her over, his eyes on mine, asking if it's safe.

"She might not give her back," I warn.

It's too late. Grandma's arms have snaked around the baby and she's pulled her away from him, bouncing her and cooing in the poor little thing's face. I couldn't stand that kind of attention from the Droning Crone, but the kid seems to love it.

"So that's your cousin?" I ask Paul.

"Mirabelle," he says, and nods sheepishly.

"Adam!" I call over the din in the kitchen. "Your date's here!"

Nancy snorts at this.

"So what's everyone doing in the kitchen?" Paul asks, standing much closer than most people stand next to me. This must be one of the signals Xander was talking about that means he wants to kiss me. It takes a little effort, but I stay where I am, standing close. I can smell the soap on his skin. Nice clean white soap.

"We're waiting for Margot to bring Xander through the front door," I tell him, "and then we're all supposed to rush into the living room yelling 'Happy birthday.'"

"I won't let you down, captain!" He salutes.

We smile a little goofily, until Dad comes up to us. "So I see you have tracked down my daughter."

"'Tracked down' might be overstating things. I left a note, she called."

Dad's eyes narrow, and he takes a long, speculative sip on his hard cider. "Okay then."

"This is *Paul,* Dad," I say, to force him to be nicer.

"Pleased to meet you properly, Paul," Dad says, offering him his hand to shake. "Soda?" He points at the fridge.

"Sure!" Paul gets two bottles of ginger ale and opens them both, handing one to me. This seems to soften Dad up, and he saunters away to go talk to Nancy, who is telling Neil a very loud story about the time she hit a BMW while trying to parallel park her junky Civic. She got out of the car only to find she had rear-ended the mayor. Neil roars with laughter. Grandma takes a break from cooing at little Mirabelle to shush him, then Dad yells, "You forgot to tell him your registration had lapsed!"

"What's going on?"

We all turn to see Xander standing in the kitchen doorway, her arms folded over her braless chest. She's wearing her flannel pajama bottoms, and her hair is sticking up in a mess of tangles. "I could hear you all the way across the street!"

The entire room shushes, except for Mirabelle, who says, "Ucky?"

We all burst out with, "Happy birthday!!!" and rush at her. She backs into the living room, totally shocked, and that's when Margot comes in the front door looking confused. Behind her are two guys, both of them wearing jeans and clean T-shirts, which for them, I think, must be the same as dressing up.

"Happy birthday!" Margot cries, jumping up and down, bracing herself on the shoulder of the guy who I guess must be her boyfriend. With his greased black hair and pierced bottom lip, he's not really what I think of as cute, though I guess he has a kind of animal magnetism. There's something about his joyless smile that I don't like.

The other guy is cute, and he steps toward Xander. "I'm Topher. Happy birthday." His hair is a nice clean strawberry color, and he has lots of freckles on his nose and forehead. As he shakes hands with Xander, I can tell he thinks she's hot even though it's clear she hasn't even showered today.

Xander narrows her eyes at Margot, who tosses her enormous hair. "Happy birthday!" she says again, grabbing Xander's arm.

Out of the corner of my eye, I see Adam take a step forward, his eyes fixed angrily on something. I follow his gaze and realize that he's looking at Margot's boyfriend. For a second I don't understand why, but then it hits me.

It's Frank. It's the guy I kicked in the head.

The one who tried to drag Xander into his car. He shaved off his goatee. That's why I didn't recognize him at first.

Xander looks at us, unsteady, as she realizes we've recognized him. Adam shakes his head, furious, and melts back into the kitchen. Nancy rushes forward to make everyone at ease. As she cries, "Everyone grab a plate and dish up some food!" she puts a casual hand on Frank's shoulder.

He looks at her with cool dark eyes and smiles.

The Same Mistakes

THERE'S SOMETHING CARNIVOROUS in the way Frank looks at Xander. He has his arm around Margot the entire time, but it's Xander he wants. He licks his lips as he watches her blow out the candles on the birthday cake.

"Speech! Speech!" Paul yells. Mirabelle, who he's holding on his hip, claps her chubby little hands. She has no idea what a speech is, but she can tell Paul wants one, and that's enough for her.

Dad holds up his third hard cider of the night and calls to Xander, "Let's hear from our future Caltech graduate, Alexandra Vogel!"

Dad is wearing a fresh shirt tucked into khaki pants. His hair is long, but he slicked it back from his forehead, and though he's gained about fifteen pounds in the last year, he's my dad. He looks like he's having a great time too. Nancy keeps smiling at him over her hard cider, and I can tell she's as happy as I am that he isn't acting like he's waiting for the world to end.

"Hear, hear!" Nancy cries, and burps. "Speech!"

Even Neil stops talking to Grandma and turns to look at Xander. Adam creeps out of the kitchen, where he's been hiding, and smolders at her.

"Okay, you pathetic losers. You'll get your speech." Xander puts down her slice of cake and wipes her frosting-covered fingers on her pajama bottoms. She takes her place at the center of the room and smiles graciously. "When I was a little girl, I wanted to be a pole dancer. There was something about the tassels, the glitter, the body paint. I don't know. It spoke to me."

Nancy snorts at this. Dad buries his face in one hand in mock horror. Grandma sniffs and turns away.

Paul looks at me wryly as if to ask, *Is she always like this?*

I shrug.

"I hit puberty," Xander continues, "but my breasts never did, and I realized that pole dancing wasn't in the cards for me. After a long grieving process, I unzipped my go-go boots, as it were, and slipped into a lab coat and protective goggles. In short, I'm geeking up."

"Thank Christ for that," Dad says.

"And now I will perform an interpretive dance that depicts my journey from aspiring pole dancer to hopeful particle physicist . . ." She gives Dad a teasing look. "Or maybe I'll just quit while I'm ahead."

"I was hoping for the dance," Frank says, and Margot elbows him in the stomach.

Xander glances at him and looks away as though she never saw him. He raises one eyebrow, trying to look cool, but he seems stirred up.

"Anyway, folks." Her eyes are suddenly shiny, and she says through a reedy voice, "I wasn't looking forward to my first birthday without Mom, but I'm glad you guys did this. Thanks."

Nancy rushes up to give Xander a hug, spilling cider on her shirt in the process. Xander laughs loudly, and people start chatting again. Topher, the guy Margot brought, leans close to Xander and gives her a farm-boy smile. She nods at him uncomfortably. He's cute, but I can tell she doesn't like him.

"Isn't that the guy you went to the prom with?" Paul asks, and I turn to see him looking at Adam, vaguely threatened.

"Yeah, that's my neighbor. He's kind of our best friend."

"He seems kind of . . ."

"Like he wants to kill someone?"

Adam's eyes are fixed on Frank with a predatory stare.

"Yeah."

"He does."

"Okay. Fair enough." Paul grins, and I notice the tiny whiskers on his upper lip are pale brown, like the hair on his arms.

"Want cake?" I ask.

"I was born wanting cake! But I need to sit down for a minute. She's heavier than she looks." He lowers himself onto the sofa next to Neil and Grandma, who immediately crowds herself around Mirabelle again, cooing, "Who's the little cutie pie! Who's the little muffin? Is that you? Are you the little muffin?"

I sidle up to Nancy's dining room table, and I'm bumped from behind. I turn to see Frank staring at me. Until now, he's acted like he didn't recognize me at all. I figured he was too drunk that night to really remember me. Or maybe I kicked him in the head too hard.

"Hi," he says in an edgy voice.

"Hello," I say. I look over at Margot, who is trying hard to get Xander to like the blond guy. She's saying, "See, you're Xander, short for Alexandra, and he's Topher, short for Christopher! I thought you two just had to meet!"

Frank pulls a toothpick out of his mouth and points it at me. "Do I know you?"

"No," I say.

He waits for me to elaborate, but I don't. I busy myself with cutting two big slices of cake, and I back away from him with the plates held to my stomach. I don't like his metallic eyes. I turn my back on him and head to Paul on the couch.

"Do you want me to hold her while you eat your cake?" Grandma asks him, already lifting Mirabelle off his lap. The baby kicks at Grandma's legs until she's comfortable, and then she snuggles into the crook of her elbow, looking sleepy.

I sit on the arm of the couch next to Paul and give him his cake. "Who's that guy?" he asks warily, nodding in Frank's direction.

"Margot's boyfriend, I guess," I say.

He doesn't seem to taste his cake as he studies Frank's black jeans and tattoos and unlaced sneakers. "He doesn't seem to fit here. Everyone else is so nice, but he's so . . ."

"Oily."

"There's something not right about him."

"What is it, do you think?" I ask, not because I want to find out about Frank, but because I want to find out about Paul. I like the way he sees things.

Paul watches Frank snake one arm around Margot and nuzzle her neck with his nose. "It's like he's *pretending* to like being with people. He's pretending to have fun."

To try to see what Paul sees, I watch Frank. He has one hand tucked into the front pocket of his jeans, and he's listening to Margot talk, but he's always a beat behind. When Margot says something, he has to ask her what she said, then he laughs a little too late.

Paul is right. He's pretending.

"Poor guy," Paul says.

"Why do you say that?"

"Because he knows. He's not really welcome here."

I look around the room. Nancy is sipping from a mug, standing not three feet away from Frank. She has her head down, and she's watching him from the corner of her eye. Dad is standing by the kitchen talking to Adam, and they both keep glancing over at Frank. He is making everyone here nervous.

Xander comes over and sits on the coffee table in front of Paul. "I'm Zen's big sister." Now, more than ever, I wish my sister would wear a damn bra.

"Nice to meet you," Paul says, and shakes her hand. I like the way he is friendly to her, but a little aloof too. It's a way of being nice to me.

"Can I see you on the porch?" Xander asks me.

"Sure," I say. I put my cake down on the end table and follow her out. We sit in the porch swing, and she gets it going with one slippered foot.

"Thanks oh so much for this surprise party," she says, and pinches my shoulder.

"It's not my fault you never bothered to get dressed today!"

"I'm fully clothed."

"And what the hell about Margot's boyfriend? Huh?"

She jabs her finger in my face. "Don't you breathe a word of that to her!"

"I won't. *I* wouldn't want to hurt her."

"I'm not going into it with you, so you can keep your judgmental crap to yourself."

The screen door wheezes open, and Adam comes out. "What the hell is that creep doing here, Xander?"

"I didn't invite him."

"He's with Margot!"

"Yeah. So?" She bolts off the porch swing. "It's not like we messed around. I accepted a ride home from him."

"Xander, come on." Adam takes Xander's shoulders and shakes her, gently. "You have got to get yourself under control."

"Or what?" She practically spits the words in his face.

"God!" I yell. "I'm sick to death of you two fighting all the time."

"Who cares?" Xander takes a cigarette out of the pocket of her pajama pants and taps it on the back of a matchbook. Adam throws up his hands and marches back into the house.

"Since when do you smoke?" I ask her.

"I sometimes smoke. So what?" She lights the cigarette and draws in deeply. "Oh, that's good."

"It smells like rancid incense."

She ignores me, and sits down on the top porch step. She kisses the cigarette quietly, tracing the blue smoke with her eyes as it floats up to mingle with the tree branches above her. "I got another letter," she says quietly. "Came with the gas bill."

"What does it say?"

She pulls it out of the rear pocket of her flannel pants and hands it to me. She laughs, as though trying to discredit it.

Dear Xander,

Happy birthday, my sweetheart! I hope that you're celebrating and enjoying yourself today.

You are, by now, preparing yourself for college. I ordered you a nice wool blazer for your birthday. It is a professional-looking jacket, and it will look good with jeans. It should be arriving this week. Now that you're a college woman, I thought you might like to look the part a little. Gabardine never fails.

Knowing you, I'm sure that you'll conquer college just like you conquer everything else. I do want to warn you, though, honey, that your professors might not respond as indulgently to your big personality as your high school teachers have. A small amount of reserve in this arena might serve you well.

You're like me in this way. You hold back when you should declare yourself, and you're flamboyant where you should be still. Sweetheart, don't make the same mistakes I've made. Don't sell yourself short professionally. Work your tail off in undergrad so that you can get your Ph.D. And don't shortchange yourself personally, either. A lot of people get only one love. Don't squander it.

I love you, my beautiful little hellion,
Mom

I fold it back up, careful not to make any new creases, and hand it back to her.

"What do you think that means?" she asks me darkly. "Don't make the same mistakes?"

I have to swallow around the big lump in my throat. "I don't want to take it apart with you, Xander."

She sits back down on the swing and whispers through smoky breath, "Do you think it means she regretted marrying Dad?"

"I don't know." I look through Nancy's lace curtains at Dad, who is leaning against the kitchen doorway, nodding uncomfortably at Neil, who is telling him some story about being a mechanic. "She always seemed pretty happy with him, didn't she?"

"Yeah, she did." She takes a long drag on her cigarette before flicking ash into a flowerpot. "I just wish I knew what it meant."

This makes me very angry. "It doesn't matter what it means, Xander. That letter isn't even to you anymore."

"What the hell does *that* mean?" Xander looks pale and hard, so far from who she was a year ago.

I want to hurt her. Maybe then she'll wake up out of this awful nightmare she's become.

"That letter was written to the old Xander, before you started going out every night, and smoking, and doing drugs, and sleeping around." I measure my words like gunpowder. "If Mom came back alive today, she wouldn't even recognize you."

I expect Xander to scream at me, but she doesn't. She just rolls her eyes, laughs, and throws her burning cigarette into the rose-bushes before marching back inside.

It takes me five minutes to find it, smoldering in dry leaves.

When I get back inside, I find the party already breaking up. "What's going on?" I ask Xander, who is gathering paper plates.

"I'm going home to get dressed, and then Margot and I have an-other party to go to," Xander says. She straightens, a teasing glint in her eye. "Want to come?" she asks, knowing that I won't. I hate par-ties like the one she's talking about, where there are tons of people I don't know expecting me to act the way they act, drink what they drink, and measure myself by how they treat me. If she thought there was a chance in hell I'd take her up on the invitation, she'd never have offered it. Which really makes me mad.

"Hmm. Maybe I will come along," I say, just to tease her. "If Paul can."

"I can come," Paul says eagerly. "I just have to drop off Mirabelle first."

Adam steps forward, his eyes hard. "That's a great idea. Let's all go see what Xander does in her spare time."

Xander narrows her eyes angrily at him, but she tosses her hair, the picture of nonchalance. "Fine. Sounds like a great time," she says.

All the while, Frank is watching our conversation with determined eyes.

The Other Party

That's how Adam, Paul, and I ended up sitting on a scratchy log, watching Xander and Margot take beer bong hits under a canopy of stars somewhere in the deep Vermont woods. Topher is holding the girls as they lean backwards, and Frank is pouring the beer down their throats. As he fits the nozzle into Xander's mouth, Frank looks at her almost tenderly. It's a weird combination to force a liter of beer down someone's throat with gentleness. It doesn't match up.

"Booyah!" Xander yells as she wipes the beer from her chin.

I can tell Xander thinks she's being naughty and interesting. That she's sexy like this. But I watch Adam as he watches her weaving around, and there's nothing in his eyes but disgust.

She *is* disgusting like this. Beer has spilled down her shirt, which sticks to her skin in a mess of wrinkles. Her jeans are hanging on her hips, making her look sloppy. She can't walk straight, and she's trying to act cool, but her performance is false and sad. Everyone else at the party is watching her, but not with admiration. They're laughing at her.

For the first time in my entire life, I am ashamed of my sister. She is turning into a loser, and she isn't doing anything to stop herself.

"Oh. Just a sec," Xander says, and stumbles over to lean on a tree while she throws up. She sounds like an animal. "There went my birthday cake," she slurs. She's trying to be funny, but no one laughs, except Margot, who doubles over and stumbles into Topher, who seems only too willing to catch her.

"So, this is a great party," Paul says, and takes a tiny sip of vile wine. I'm sipping beer, but I don't like the taste of it. I'm not even sure I should be drinking alcohol with all the Motrin I've been taking. I probably shouldn't even be here. My back is aching, and I want to go home, but Adam is our ride and he isn't showing any signs of letting up his watch over Xander.

I look around at the other people here. There are about a dozen pickup trucks parked around the gravel pit. We must be somewhere near the quarry in Barre, and we're surrounded by mountains of white sand piled high. There are ghosts of dump trucks parked in the shadows, and I can't help imagining sinister men behind the wheels, watching us.

I don't know any of the other people here, but they all seem to know Xander. Judging from the girls, this must be where she gets her recent fashion sense. They're all wearing ripped jeans that are too tight, and skimpy tank tops without bras, and studded belts, and ankle boots or platform sandals. They look to be in high school, but there's something used up about them, like they've already done too much living.

Xander stumbles over to us, a stupid smile on her face. "Hey, guys. Having fun?"

"Sure," Paul says. He's trying to sound sincere for my sake, but I can tell he's as nervous about being here as I am.

"How much longer do you plan to stay?" I ask Xander.

"It's my birthday" is all she says, and she weaves away, kicking up gravel. She turns her ankle and almost falls over, but Frank catches her.

"I don't like this," Adam says.

Another pickup drives up. The heavy beat of a bass guitar vibrates through its metal as it parks right in front of us. People shout hello, and flock over to it. From the driver's seat emerges a short man with a slant of brown hair on his head. He's wearing a denim jacket, and his jeans look two sizes too big for him. There's a huge smile on his face, and he shouts, "Who wants to get happy!" People crowd around him, and he starts taking money with one hand and handing out tiny paper envelopes with the other.

"Oh, shit," Adam says.

"What is that?" Paul asks me. He's scared now.

He's going to think I'm some kind of horrible, drug-abusing slut-cake. "Paul, I've never been to a party like this in my life."

"Your sister has."

I follow his gaze to see Xander triumphantly walking away from the circle of people, holding one of the envelopes.

I bolt off the log, but I don't get to her as quickly as Adam does. He pulls her by the elbow away from the glare of headlights, leaning close to her, speaking soft and vicious. "What the hell is that?"

"It's fine!" Xander yells, and jerks her arm out of his grip.

"What's going on here?" Frank says to Adam as he slicks a hand over his oily black hair, like he's some authority figure and Adam is some abuser of women. He must think backwards like this all the time. "Let go of her."

Adam ignores him. "Just stop, okay, Xander? Stop and take a look at what you're doing!"

"Oh god, what a cliché!" She throws back her head and laughs like she's howling at the moon.

"Xander," I say. I advance toward her. "If you take whatever's in that envelope, I swear to you, I'll tell Dad."

This sobers her up. "Don't you dare, you little—"

"She's right." I turn to see that Margot is standing right behind me, her hands on her hips. "You told me, you *promised* me, you'd never try that stuff again, Xander."

I never expected this. I thought Margot was the one pulling Xander into her spiral, but now I see maybe it's the other way around. Topher is standing next to Margot uncertainly, watching the scene, his pretty blue eyes scrunched in confusion. He looks at Frank like he needs a cue about how to act. When he sees the deadly steel in Frank's eyes, he hardens up too.

I look at Paul, who has stood up from the log and is watching the scene warily. He glances at me, and his eyes tell me that whatever happens, he'll back me up.

I really like that guy.

"Let's just go, okay?" Adam pulls on Xander's arm again.

Xander yells, "No!" just as Frank steps forward and says through his teeth, "I said let go of her."

Frank throws down the beer bong angrily and it cracks against the gravel.

The party goes quiet.

I feel a dull sting in my palm and realize that I've been standing in strike pose, fists clenched, my fingernails digging into my skin.

Suddenly Adam wraps his arms around Xander, and he's nuzzling her hair, whispering at her. "Please don't do this. Please, Xander. You've got to come back to us. Please?"

He leans his head down on her shoulder and rests it there.

Her voice is cold crystal shards. "Why are you *crying?*"

Adam lifts his head and looks in her eyes. "My god, Xander. *Why aren't you?*"

Her whole body jerks straight as a lightning rod, and for a second all she can do is look at him. Her mouth is open, her eyes defensive, her hands working into fists and out again as she tries to think of what to say. Finally she scoffs and pulls away from him.

Adam points at the envelope she's holding. "Xander, this isn't you."

"It's just X, Adam," she says weakly.

"Come home, Xander," he says. He takes a careful step toward her and gently works the envelope from between her fingers and drops it on the ground.

I glance at Frank, who doesn't seem to understand anything

about what Adam is doing. "Listen," he says, "she doesn't want to go home," like he's defending her rights.

"Oh, shut up, Frank," she says. "You don't know what I want." She casts a shameful look at Margot, who is staring at the ground. Margot can't have missed Frank's possessiveness over Xander, and she must understand what it means.

Xander's eyes travel all around, and her face changes.

Everyone is watching us.

I forgot they were even here.

The guy who came with the ecstasy takes a few short steps toward us. "Hey, there's no need to cause a stink about this."

Adam walks right by him, pulling on Xander, who finally starts to follow him, her head down, face looking confused. "Let's go."

"I said let the girl go." Frank squares himself against Adam, a threat in his eyes.

"It's fine, Frank," Xander says, resigned. "Leave it."

"No. This guy shouldn't be pushing you around."

"He's not," I hear Paul say, and turn to see him reaching a hand toward Frank to try to reason with him. Everything about Paul is cool and calm, but he's tall, much taller than Frank, who takes a step back from him. He doesn't understand what Paul is trying to do. Paul takes another step toward Frank, and another. "Adam just wants—"

Out of nowhere, Frank's fist shoots into Paul's face, and suddenly Paul is sprawled flat on the ground, dazed.

I'm aiming my foot at Frank's chest before I even register how mad I am. And I *am* mad. All the pain and frustration and rage of the past year courses through me as I fly through the air toward Frank. When my foot crashes into him, it feels so good, I have to smile.

He falls down so easily underneath me, it's almost like I'm dreaming about this. Before he can catch his breath, I'm in strike pose again, and I stand over him, ignoring my screaming back, my foot poised directly above his larynx. "Adam, get the car," I say.

Then I'm grabbed from behind.

"What do you think you're doing to my friend?" I hear the words spat into my ear. The breath is warm and harsh.

"Leave her alone!" Margot screams.

I try to drop down as I've been trained to do, Release from Bear Hug, but my back is twisting and pulling apart, and no matter how I move I can't relieve the pressure on my spine. I make myself breathe steadily, and from the corner of my eye I see who's holding me.

It's Topher, the meek little farm boy. He's holding me like they hold calves when they're branding them. He tightens his grip and I scream.

It hurts so much. "Please. My back" is all I can say.

"Let her go," I hear Xander growl. I've never heard her sound so dangerous.

"Did you see what she did to Frank?" he says, his voice cracking like a little boy's.

"Please. You're hurting me," I whimper.

I've never felt like this.

I've never been helpless.

His arms clamp together even harder.

I cry out. Tubes of pain stretch and twist all through my spine. It's a deep, terrible sting, like Mom said.

"Just relax," Mom whispers at me. *"He doesn't want to hurt you."*

"Let her go," Xander says, "or I swear to Christ I'll kill you."

She says it calmly, like she's stating a simple fact. I glance at her, and I see she's holding a rock in her fist.

For the first time, his grip loosens a little. The small motion sends diamonds of pain all through me.

I hear a footstep behind, and suddenly I'm dropped to the ground. I roll over on my back and look up to see Adam and Topher struggling with each other. Adam's arm is wrapped around Topher's neck, and they're both red-faced and ugly. I want to help. I should help, but I can't move.

Topher can't get out of Adam's grip, so he rakes his fingernails down Adam's arm. Adam screams, and then I see a rising dark shape, and I'm so scared, because I think it's Frank, but then I see shiny hair. It's Paul. He's walking toward the both of them, and he's speaking very softly, his hands held out in front of him. "Calm down, guys. Okay? Just calm down."

Both of them are looking at him, breathing hard.

"Topher. How about this?" Paul's voice is perfectly steady, but I can see his fingertips are quaking like leaves on a tree. "How about if you nod, it means that when Adam lets you go, you let us walk away. We'll leave. And we won't come back. And nobody has to go to the hospital tonight, or explain anything to the cops. Okay? Does that work for you?"

All the innocent farm-boy looks are gone from Topher. He's raging, breathing so hard that snot is flying from his nose, spit from his mouth. His eyes are hooded and furious, like a dog's.

I hear a shuffle to my left, and I move my head to see that Frank is trying to get up. This sends a jolt of fear through me, and I pull myself up to lean against Margot. "I gotcha," she says. Frank eyes me as he rubs his chest, half sitting up and leaning on his elbow.

"Adam," Paul says, "maybe Topher can't nod because you're holding his head too tight. How about you loosen up a little so he can nod his head, and we can all communicate, okay?"

Adam's eyes are cold, but I can see he's thinking, reasoning through this. He sees Paul is right. There's only one way out of this that doesn't end with jail, or worse. "Okay." I can't see a change in the way he's holding Topher, but Topher feels the change because suddenly he's taking in huge gulps of air.

"Okay. So Topher?" Paul waits until Topher looks him in the eye, and then he continues. "So you're going to let us walk away, right? When Adam lets you go?"

He seems to think about it for a second. Then he nods once.

"Okay. I'm going to count to three, and that's when you let him go, Adam. One."

Topher shifts his feet.

"Two."

Adam braces himself with his legs.

"Three."

Adam lets go of Topher.

Topher breaks Adam's nose with the heel of his hand.

A scream peals through the night, and Xander is running to Adam, who has dropped to his knees, his head lolling. She runs to him, kneels by him, takes his hand. She whispers, "I'm sorry I'm sorry I'm sorry."

Topher walks calmly over to the keg, pumps out two cups of beer, and brings one over to Frank, who is sitting all the way up now.

"Can you walk?" Paul says, and cups his hand to my face. "Can you get to the car?"

"I'll bring it around," Margot says. She shifts me over to lean against Paul, then jogs to Adam and Xander and gets the keys, jogs away.

A couple people from the party, including the guy who brought the ecstasy, come over to me and Paul. "She going to be all right?"

I want to shrug it off. I don't like people looking at me like this. But I can't speak because it's all hitting me. How crazy Xander is. How dangerous these people are. How badly Adam and I are hurt. How gone Mom is. I want my *mom*.

"I don't know," I hear Paul say. He rubs my back, presses his lips to my forehead, breathes into my hair.

Adam's car pulls up. Paul and the drug dealer hook their hands under my armpits, and slowly, gently, they raise me to my feet. Standing hurts a whole lot less than lying down. They lower me slowly into the back seat, then Xander brings Adam and lowers him in next to me. His eyes are screwed closed. His nose is crooked and bleeding, and it's clear he's hurting, but he'll be fine. Paul gets in the passenger seat, Margot takes the wheel, and Xander gets in behind Margot. It seems like we're almost away, but then the worst possible thing happens.

Frank leans into the driver's side window and gives me a vicious glare. "I'm not finished with you, little girl."

I'm terrified, until Margot reaches into Frank's mouth with one clawed finger and hooks his cheek so that he has to look at her. "I'm finished with *you*, Frank. And if you come after *anyone* in this car, I'll slap you with a statutory rape charge so fast, your head will spin." His face slackens, and he holds his hands up in surrender. He's trying to put a mocking expression on his face, but I can tell what Margot said shook him up. She hits the window control so that it rolls up, almost catching Frank's cheek with it before she lets it go.

"Sweetie," Frank pleads through the glass. "There's no need to get crazy." He's working hard to sound calm and steady, but there's such a look of fear in his eyes, I can see him for what he really is—a loser who can't get a woman his own age. Suddenly he's not so scary. "I lost my temper, that's all. I wouldn't hurt her! Don't go to the cops, okay, honey?"

"I mean it!" Margot snaps. "Stay away from us, or I'll throw the book at you!"

Just before we drive away between the sheltering mounds of rock, I hear the drug dealer ask Frank, incredulous, "You had *sex* with that little girl?"

The Aftermath

We get a lot of speeches.

Dad, standing over the three of us as we shrink into the sofa: "A black belt in shotokan is not a license to start fights! And you, Xander! You have everything going for you. A full ride to Caltech. And here you are, risking everything on a tablet of ecstasy! My god, what have you become!"

Nancy pacing the porch while we sit in her rickety swing: "What were you kids *doing* at a party like that? In the middle of nowhere? Drugs? Booze? Have you seen Adam's face lately? He looks like he got stepped on by a moose!"

Grandma on the phone: "You're children, the both of you! When I was your age, I was learning to crochet doilies with my girl-friends! We danced in the basement to old seventy-eights! We were innocent! You can never get that back! *Never!*"

Aunt Doris on the phone: "At least marijuana is *natural.* You can even grow it yourself. But those designer drugs are dangerous! Just one mistake in the lab, and suddenly your brains are scrambled eggs! Oh, I should have hidden my stash better! This is all my fault!"

After the speeches, everyone took a break from one another for a few days. Dad went back to hide in the basement, though I hear him outside our bedroom doors a lot more often. He's been knock-ing, and calling tersely, "You in there?" We always answer yes, and he always says, "Good. Because you're still grounded."

I hear Xander going to the bathroom and then back to her room. She doesn't even play her stereo. I hear her tapping on her keyboard a lot, though.

I've been flat on my back for almost a week. Now my back is sprained in two places instead of just one. I'm under orders to get up and walk around once every hour, and I do, but the first few steps feel like I'm getting sprained all over again. It's awful to be hurt. It's awful to know that the person who did it is out there, and he probably isn't even sorry.

I have nightmares about being held down. Something is behind me, twisting my body, and I can't see what it is, but I can feel its strength. I wake up breathing hard, my throat dry and my sheets soggy. It isn't an easy thing to get over feeling helpless.

I hear a tap on my door, and it swings open to reveal Xander. She has her hair in two braids pinned to the top of her head, and she's wearing Mom's old overalls and a black T-shirt. It's a shock to see her like this, because she looks like she did a year ago, before Mom died. She looks like the old Xander.

Maybe it was a good thing Adam wanted to go to that party after all.

"Hey," she says, and smiles wanly. "How's your back?"

"It's getting better."

She comes in and sits at the foot of my bed. "Have you talked to Adam lately?"

"No. You haven't?"

She shakes her head. There's a weak look in her eyes, and I realize she's too ashamed to call him. "I saw Nancy weeding her flower bed yesterday, and she says his black eyes are almost gone and the swelling is much better."

"Is she still mad?"

"Yeah, but I think she's proud of him too. The way he tried to defend us."

"You should call him."

"I will." She lies back on my bed, resting her head against the wall. "Do you think you could maybe travel sometime soon?" she asks.

"The doctor said I should be mostly better in about two weeks." I hope he's right. I'm so sick of my back being out, I could scream.

I'd hoped she'd let this go, but of course she can't. The truth is, I've been thinking about John Phillips too. I want to let it go, but it won't let go of me.

"Do you think the hatchback would make it a thousand miles?" she asks, only half serious.

I make a face.

"You're right. The hatchback is out. Maybe we can borrow Dad's Audi."

"Yeah, right."

"I'll tell him it's our last chance to do a sister-on-sister road trip. He might let us."

"Ask him if we can host an orgy first. Soften him up."

This conversation is pointless. We both know Xander is planning on going with or without permission.

Her eyes slip over to my window, and I can see she's looking at Adam's house again. There's something different about her now. I've never seen her humbled, but that's how she seems. I've always admired her daring, but I like this humbled Xander too. She doesn't scare me as much. I hope she stays this way.

"If you don't go over there and talk to him," I tell her, "it's going to seem like you don't care."

"I know." She stands up, patting down the overalls, which are huge on her. "How do I look?"

"Like my sister."

She takes a deep breath and slowly walks to the door. "Wish me luck." She turns to look at me over her shoulder. She's biting her bottom lip so hard that it's turned white. She's afraid. She gets halfway out my bedroom door and stops, turns. "Can you come with me?"

"No, Xander."

"Zen. I don't know what to say."

"The truth usually works on people. Maybe you should try that for once."

She stands there, staring at the rug in front of her feet. "I'm not sure what the truth *is*."

"In another month you guys are going off to college, and if you don't take care of it soon, things can never be put back the way they were."

"Oh, Zen. That's already true." She smiles at this, and for a second I see a glimpse of the Xander who always thinks she knows what's best. "We'll never be the same again."

She closes the door behind her, but I can hear her standing on the noisy floorboard in the hall. It squawks under her, as though she's shifting her weight back and forth. Finally I hear her footsteps, slow and halting, as they go back into her room.

Coward.

I want to close my eyes for a nap, but I'm too haunted by the memory of Topher's arms clamped around me, holding me helpless while I screamed in pain. It sends a searing ache through my guts, and I fold into myself.

I lie still, imagining pulling out of Topher's hold and kicking him in the head. I kick him harder and harder in my mind until I hear his neck snap. Now instead of feeling helpless, I feel sick to my stomach.

I think there's something wrong with me, deep inside.

I ease myself out of bed, hobble out to the hallway, and pick up the phone.

He answers on the second ring. "Shotokan, Sensei speaking."

"Mark, it's Zen."

"Hi! How are you doing?"

The question completely undoes me, and I start crying. I try to be silent about it, but even my silence gives me away. Finally Mark asks, voice low, "What happened?"

I tell him the whole story, starting at the surprise party, and then describing how Frank punched Paul, and how I had launched myself at Frank before I'd even had time to think. I tell him how I'd been held against my will, how I'm haunted by that, and how helpless I feel about everything.

When I'm done, he's silent for a long time. Finally, he speaks, but he sounds shaky. "So what do you think you're learning from this?"

"I don't know," I tell him. "I was hoping you'd be able to help me."

"When you attacked, did you use your skill to good purpose?"

I say nothing, because trying to defend myself would sound to him like I'm not learning anything. The truth is, I'm not sure what I'm supposed to learn.

He senses my hesitation, and his tone changes. "Zen, I think you need to do your soul-searching on your own. This isn't something I can teach."

"Okay." My eyes trace the outlines of my room, and I try to think of something more to say.

"We're adding another intermediate section in the fall. The class starts September fifteenth. Can you make it?"

He's not really asking me if I *want* to. He's asking if I'll sort through my baggage by then. "I'll try."

"It will be great to have you back. We've missed you."

I feel incredibly tired. After we hang up, I dig under my covers and close my eyes, letting myself fall asleep.

LECTURE FROM MOM

I WAKE TO FIND MOM playing in the dappled light that moves through the tree leaves outside my bedroom window. They flutter, and she speaks. "A black belt doesn't make you invincible."

"I know." I turn my head and breathe in the scent of my fresh pillowcase, which Xander brought up this morning.

"Besides, it's only a lower-grade black belt. You're not a master."

"I know."

"A master could've gotten away from that Topher kid, hurt back or no hurt back."

"I know, Mom!"

"And now here you are, staring at the crack in the ceiling, talking to your dead mother, who is very angry with you."

"I was defending my friend!"

"You escalated an already violent situation," she says.

"What do you want? Want me to prostrate myself and beg for forgiveness?"

"You're already prostrate, and no. I just want you to learn this lesson. You've been pushing your body too far. Every time you're almost better, you do something to hurt yourself again."

"You know, Xander's the one who got us into this."

"Xander's unraveling in her way, you're unraveling in yours."

"I'm the only one in the family who's held it together!"

"Oh yeah? How many fights did you get in *before* I died?"

This stops me. For a second I forget that I'm having a fight with Mom, and I just think. This is what Mark meant when he asked if I'd used my skill to good purpose. Maybe I wasn't really protecting my friends so much as looking for an excuse to let my anger out.

Even if Mom has a point, that doesn't mean I have to admit anything. "Xander's still acting crazier than I am. I don't know why you're not lecturing her!"

"Oh, she's getting a lecture, all right."

"You talk to her? Because she insists there's no such thing as ghosts."

"Hey! I resent that. I'm a spirit, not a ghost!"

"What's the difference?"

"This is not a haunting."

"Okay. Whatever."

I open my eyes to the lines of light on the ceiling drawn there by my blinds. Particles of dust float, twinkling, and I imagine that Mom is one of them, floating around, enjoying her weightlessness.

"What's it like to be dead?"

"It's apart. I'm apart. But I'm here."

"Like you're on the other side of a wall?"

"More like I'm on the other side of time."

"What does it feel like?"

"Like I'm underwater, or in an envelope of water, and I'm looking at all of you moving around in the air. I'm held by the water, I'm part of the water, and I can't get out of it, but it's soothing, and warm, and it feels nice. So I've learned to accept it."

"I wish I could see you."

"I know." I feel a whisper of air against my cheek, and I imagine that she has kissed me. "Your father is coming out of his funk."

"Yeah. He looks much better."

"You guys are going to be okay."

I watch the light cast through the shimmery leaves as it dances on my bedroom wall. Mom and I painted that wall a pale peach five summers ago, before she got sick. It was fun painting with Mom, changing the color of my room, listening to the radio as we worked. She taught me a song. "Knock three times on the ceiling if you want me." She would knock on the ceiling as she sang it, and Dad would call from downstairs for us to be quiet.

"That was a fun day," she says, her voice a wisp of shadow in my ear.

Suddenly I hate this. I hate that I have to communicate with her in fluttering leaves and shadows. It's so unfair, I want to explode something.

"You seem angry," Mom whispers.

"You're right. I'm angry at *you!*"

"Say what?"

"You lied to us! You lied to us about John Phillips!"

"It's not as bad as you're thinking."

"Why did you do it? Why did you cheat on us? Why did you have to die?"

"Well, for god's sake—I tried not to!"

"That's not good enough." I'm surprised by the sound of my voice. I didn't mean to speak aloud.

She sighs. "Honey. Honey, I'm sorry."

"I know," I say in my mind. Tears burn my eyelids. I press my fist to my forehead and stiffen up my whole body. My tense muscles fire rapid shots of pain through my spine, but I ignore it. I don't want to cry. I *won't.*

"Just let it come," Mom says, and I feel her presence moving over me, under me, smoothing me over.

But is she? Is she *really?*

Is she here with me, or is she a figment of my imagination?

"Are you real?"

Silence. Only birdsong fluttering through my window.

Of course she isn't real. I've known this for a long time. I knew her well enough when she was alive that I can imagine anything she might say to me, in any situation.

Mom isn't here.

Mom is just gone, and I can't keep doing this to myself. I can't keep imagining things that aren't there.

Everything in me releases. I turn over, my face jammed into my pillow, and I cry.

I cry alone.

INDECENT EXPOSURE

"No way. No way in hell." Dad sets down his spoon, which is still full of lukewarm, sticky oatmeal, and points in Xander's face for emphasis. "I just want to make myself clear. There is *literally no way* I'm letting you two out of my sight for the rest of the summer. And I'm certainly not loaning you my very expensive European car for a road trip to an unspecified location."

"Maine!" Xander yells. "We were thinking Maine. There. It's specified."

"Young women who engage in illicit drug use do not deserve to borrow luxury automobiles."

"Well, perhaps if I'd had adequate supervision . . ." she says, just to play the guilt card.

"Oh, so you admit you need supervision, do you?"

This shuts her up.

My turn. I rest my elbows on the worn wood of our kitchen table. "Dad, we just want to be together for a few days, just us girls, before Xander leaves for Pasadena. We're not planning on doing anything crazy."

He laughs at this. "Crazy people don't make plans. The shit flies on its own."

"So we're crazy?" Xander asks. She's trying to act offended to put Dad on the defensive, but not even this works.

"Look. It's simple. You're to stay in town for the rest of the summer." He drops his bowl in the sink, shoulders his satchel, and starts toward the door. He's been getting up at eight o'clock every morning, and he's off to the library by ten. He stays there for at least four hours, and then he comes home with a stack of books and pages of careful notes. He's working again, on an article, he says, but he has also hinted it could be the first chapter of a new book about Yeats. A critical biography, he's calling it. The color has come back to his cheeks, and he seems much more awake than he has for a long time. Our trouble at the party seemed to snap him completely out of his funk. It's nice to have him back.

"I'm sorry, girls," he says as he backs out of the door, his overgrown bangs hanging in his eyes. "I love you, but I have to say no to this."

"Well, that's full of piss," Xander spits.

"Watch your language, little miss," he shoots back, and closes the door behind him.

We're quiet. I trace a yellow patch of sunlight that slants across the table. The kitchen is bright, just like when Mom used to be alive. It's strange that I think of it that way—that it's been dark in here for almost a year, but that's how it feels. It's like the house was bathed in a gray shadow, and now that Dad's come up from the basement, the sun is allowed to come in the windows. We're moving forward through time again.

Xander drops her spoon into her shredded wheat, picks it up again, and drops it. Milk splashes out onto the blue plaid tablecloth. "Well," I begin.

"Who do we know with a car?" She raises her eyebrows.

"I don't think we should just *drive* there."

"Do what you want. I'm eighteen years old."

I did not think of that, but it's true. Technically, she's an adult. She can legally leave and there's nothing Dad can do about it. I'm a different matter, though. "He might never forgive us if we defy him."

"He'll forgive us. He has to. He's our dad."

We're quiet for a long time while we think. When the kitchen starts to get hot from the sun, we move onto the front porch and sit on the creaky wicker chairs. I put my hand on the armrest and it comes away with a spider web stuck to my fingers. I ball up the fibers and try to flick them away, but they keep clinging to me.

I hear a door slam and look to see that Adam has come out of his house. He still has the pale blue splint on his face to protect his nose. He notices us and freezes. Out of the corner of my eye I see Xander straightening up. We stare at each other like that until I finally wave at him to break the spell. "How's your nose?" I call.

He shrugs. "Okay. Not great."

"Will it heal purdy?" Xander asks him in her hillbilly accent.

The tension evaporates. He half smiles, and slowly crosses the street. As he comes up our porch stairs I see that the bruises under his eyes are faded to yellow. "The doctor says it was a clean break. It should heal okay."

"That's good," Xander says. She gives him a shy smile.

I have to look at her again.

Yes, I would definitely characterize the smile on her face as a shy one. Demure, even.

Adam smiles at her too, but his smile is sad. Wistful.

"So, know anywhere we can steal a car?" Xander asks him.

He raises one eyebrow at her. "Already breaking the law again?"

"Adam." She pauses for a moment, her eyes soulful and deadly earnest. "I can't go to college without putting this thing to rest."

His smile fades. He thoughtfully scratches at the tip of his nose, just under the splint. "You know, my dad has an extra car."

This gets her attention. "Would it make it a thousand miles?"

"Yeah. He uses it on the weekends for road trips. I'm sure it would be fine."

"Would he loan it to you?" I ask.

"He cut my visit last month short so he could take Melissa to Hawaii." He says her name as though speaking about poison. "He feels guilty enough that he might."

For the first time since the party, Xander smiles with that devilish glint in her eyes. "Want to go to Wisconsin?"

"Have I ever told you how much cheddar cheese means to me?" he replies with a crooked smile.

The phone inside rings, and Xander pops up to get it. My back is feeling much better today, but popping up is still beyond me. Adam is looking at the tree in our yard, watching a robin on the bottom branch. It seems like the bird is watching him too. I wonder if he's remembering Beverly. He probably is. Of anyone I know, Adam cares the most. About everything.

"Thanks, Adam," I say, without stopping to think of how strange it might sound.

He looks at me quizzically.

"You brought her back," I tell him, by way of explanation.

He smiles at this, but he says nothing.

"Paul's coming over," Xander says as she slams out through the screen door.

"Thanks for asking first." I struggle out of my chair. "I need a shower."

"Hurry!" she calls after me.

At the bottom of the stairs I look back over my shoulder to see Adam taking my chair. He leans toward Xander tentatively, and she lets him.

Paul is already here when I come back down, freshly showered, in my tank top and khaki shorts. The three of them are already cooking up plans.

Paul has an atlas draped over his lap. "If you drove in shifts you could make it there in a day," he says. When he sees me, he stands up, forgetting the atlas, and it slides to the floor. "Hi."

"Hi." I take a step closer to him and brush my fingertips gently across the bruise on his cheekbone where Frank hit him. It feels so natural to touch him, I don't even notice how exhilarating it is until after I've done it. He takes my hand and holds it to his chest, smiling.

"Hey! What time is it?" Xander has stood up and is peering through the living room curtains at the mantel clock.

"We can make it," Adam says.

We all step off the porch, Paul behind us. "Where are we going?" he asks me.

"It's a tradition," I tell him. It feels so right to have Paul as part of our group, I have to grab his hand and swing it between us as we walk. I'm too happy not to.

Xander and Adam walk a lot faster than I can go, but I don't mind, because Paul hangs back with me. I've wanted to be alone with him ever since that awful night. "I never told you thanks."

"For what?"

"For what you did that night. You were so cool-headed. And"— I take in a deep breath of velvety summer air—"mature. You were mature. Much more grown up than anyone else. I just made things worse, but you got us out of there."

"Not without that bastard hurting your back," he says angrily.

"That wasn't your fault."

He nods, his eyes on Xander and Adam.

They're walking an arm's length apart, Xander's long legs moving like a dancer's as she matches her stride to his. Adam has his hands in the pockets of his jeans, and he's hanging his head as he talks to her. For the first time since Mom died, they seem to be listening to each other.

"Those two," Paul says, his eyes on them, thoughtful. "They're great."

"Great?"

"Together, I mean," he says.

I watch him for a second, his hazel eyes, the bright sun on his skin. When he looks at me, I know what he's thinking. We're great too.

We let go of each other's hands to climb the stairs on the railroad bridge. Adam and Xander are already standing there, staring at the horizon. We take our places next to them, and Paul lets his eyes wander over the rusty train cars strewn on the tracks underneath us. "This place is beautiful," he says in quiet awe. "You can see forever from here."

That's what I've always loved about the bridge over the railroad. It feels timeless to be among the treetops, and removed somehow from what happens in normal time. Looking at Paul, Xander, and Adam, their faces alight with anticipation as they watch for the train, I feel that I'm seeing their essences, who they are, or who they'll be when everything is finally stripped away and we all join Mom, wherever she is.

Xander looks at me. When I meet her eyes, she smiles.

We hear a whistle. I turn to see the train puffing toward us.

"What's on it?" Xander asks, excited.

"Coal!" I yell.

"Cars!" Adam says.

"Logs?" Paul squints at the train as it barrels toward us. "No. Those are huge pipes! HUGE! Look at how many of them!"

"Get ready!" Xander screams.

I watch her, pleading, *Please don't flash the engineer in front of Paul. Please.*

She doesn't. Instead, she turns around, facing away from the train, and pulls down her pants. "Honk if you're an ass man!" she screams.

I hear a wild laugh and turn to see Paul unbuttoning his jeans. Adam has already yanked his shorts down.

What the hell. I whip my shorts down to my knees and feel the rush of the wind on the tender skin of my ass.

Turns out Xander's right. Indecent exposure is a total rush.

THE WEE HOURS

IT'S JUST BEFORE DAWN. I'm standing on the porch with Xander, waiting for Adam to bring the car around. I look back at the house and imagine Dad finding our note, which is full of assurances that we'll be fine, that everything is okay, that he doesn't have to worry. I have a sick feeling in the bottom of my stomach about this. I know he'll be beside himself, no matter how comforting the note or how many times we call from the road.

"Stop worrying," Xander says when she sees me looking in the living room window. "We'll be back in a couple days."

"This is a bad idea."

"Then stay. Adam and I will go."

I take a half step away from her. My foot hits a hollow place in the porch, which makes a soft drum sound, too soft for Dad to hear, but I pause to listen for him anyway. Part of me wants him to come out and stop us. But I need to know the truth almost as much as she does. I need to talk to John Phillips in person too.

"No you don't," Mom murmurs in a soft whisper of tires on pavement.

It's Adam parking the car, not Mom's voice.

I've stopped listening. She isn't real, and I have to move on.

Adam pulls up in front of the house.

"Nice," Xander says.

The car is even nicer than Dad's. It looks like a cross between a sports car and a luxury sedan, with shiny blue paint and white leather seats. Adam pops the trunk and then runs over to pick up our luggage. We're traveling light, with only a couple pairs of pants and a few shirts, but our bags still barely fit in the small trunk.

We close the doors quietly, and Adam eases away from the curb. I settle in the back seat, stretched out to take the pressure off my spine. I'm almost well enough to start physical therapy, which the doctor says will make me good as new, but right now I feel fragile.

I look at Adam and Xander in the front seat, both of them squinting into the sunrise as we get on the highway. They aren't talking, but there's a kind of unity between them in the way they're sitting next to each other. It's a different kind of unity from when we three were friends. Somehow they're closer now and I'm on the outside. Looking at Xander and seeing how calm she is with Adam around, I can deal with it. I'm even a little happy about it.

Besides, now I have Paul.

He almost came with us, but at the last minute he backed out.

"It's not worth what it would put my parents through," he'd said, sitting across the table from me in the ice cream parlor where Mom and I used to go, a hot fudge sundae between us. It was the first time since Mom died that it felt right for me to be there. It used to be my place with Mom. Now it's my place with Paul. "I'll be here when you get back," he told me.

I liked the way that sounded, and I repeated it to myself later that night as I fell asleep.

"What are you going to say when we get there?" Adam asks Xander.

She cranes her neck to look at me, a quizzical expression on her face. "I have no idea."

The day goes by in a blur. First the rolling hills of Vermont and New York, then the flat lushness of Ohio and Indiana. There are tassels on the corn, miles and miles of green corn stretching out under a huge sky. So many white clouds. Then, in the evening, driving along the shores of Lake Erie, watching the metal bodies of boats dividing the water, leaving behind long streams of churning white.

I sleep in the back while the two of them drive in shifts. I hear them talking in low voices when they think I'm asleep, sharing confessions with each other. Adam whispers, "I wish I'd told you sooner how I felt."

"I wouldn't have listened," she whispers. "I knew we'd only have the summer, and I couldn't stand to lose another person."

A motion against the leather of the seat, and I open my eyes to see him stroking her yellow hair. "You won't lose me."

It's dark when we pull in to a roadside motel. Xander pays for the room while Adam and I wait around back. We all trudge up the stairwell, which is muggy with the smell of new carpet. The room is small, with a huge bed and a little sofa, onto which Adam collapses. Xander and I take the bed. It's so soft, I fall asleep immediately.

"We should get there by noon," Xander says eagerly. We're sitting in a diner, talking over our plates of eggs and enormous pancakes. Adam is hunched over a cup of coffee as though it's the only source of warmth on the planet. Xander is bleary-eyed, but a subdued excitement plays on her features. "How should we approach him?"

"Walking?" I say.

"Riding dogs?" Adam suggests.

"Zen, you're the most normal one of us."

"Hey! Adam's more normal than me!"

She looks at him askance. "Yeah, but he's not a Vogel. I think you should do the talking this time. It's delicate, and you may have noticed during our long association that delicacy is not really my . . . um . . . forte."

"Fine," I say. "Coward."

"Whatever. I'll call Dad."

She leaves the table, and Adam and I dig in to our breakfast. I've managed only a few bites of my pancake, which is pretty greasy, when she comes back looking pale.

"How'd he sound?" I ask.

"I didn't talk to him." She bumps her shoulder against Adam. "Your mom blew an aneurysm when she heard my voice."

"Great."

"She says Dad is out looking for us."

"Did you tell her we're out of town?" I ask.

"No. I hung up."

"You hung up on my mom?" Adam asks, stricken.

"Yeah. I didn't know what else to do." She seems a little disturbed, like she's only now realizing what this is doing to Dad and Nancy. It's making them crazy, and it's not fair to them.

We watch our eggs turn cold, and then the waitress brings the check. "Well, we're committed now," I say. "Let's finish this thing."

The last leg of the drive seems very short, probably because I don't really want to get to Milwaukee. I *need* to talk to Phillips, but I don't *want* to.

It's a much prettier town than I imagined, full of red brick and tall buildings. The water of Lake Michigan comes right up to the downtown where all the skyscrapers are. We roam through the city looking for the Sheffield Street address we got from directory assistance.

"Why don't we just go to the university?" Adam asks Xander.

"Classes aren't in session," she answers. "He'll be home."

We finally find Sheffield and make a right turn. The houses are all old and colonial-looking, a lot like the houses back home. But not quite. They're newer, with different plants in the gardens. I suddenly realize how far away we are from Vermont, and I get a sick feeling in my stomach. Dad must be so scared.

"There it is!" Xander yells. "Twenty-two-oh-six! Stop!"

Adam pulls over and we look at the house. It's a tall, skinny Victorian with a turret at one corner, and a wraparound porch—the kind of house Mom would have called "splendid." It's painted a dark navy blue with white trim, but the paint is peeling in places, and the lawn looks patchy.

"Yup, this is definitely the house of a literature professor," Xander declares.

She gets out, but stops when she sees something on the lawn.

It's a tricycle. A little red tricycle on its side next to the front door. "He has kids," she whispers.

It amazes me too. I don't know why, but I always pictured him alone. Knowing he has a family makes me twice as nervous. "I don't know about this," I say.

"We just drove a thousand miles!" Xander hisses. "We're doing this!"

Reluctantly I get out of the car and stand, stretching to loosen up my back. Adam turns off the engine and leans back in his seat. "I'll wait out here for you."

I thought he'd come, but Xander doesn't seem surprised at all. She just nods.

Slowly we walk up the cracked sidewalk until there's nowhere to go but up the porch steps. Then there's nothing to do but ring the doorbell. Xander jams her thumb into it, but nothing happens. "It's stuck!" she says.

She turns to look at me, and I see my own bewilderment reflected on her face. "What now?"

Crazily, I think that we can't possibly get in, and that we have no choice but to leave right away. But Xander raises her fist to the wood of the door, pauses, and finally knocks.

A squeal issues from inside, and the door swings open to reveal a little boy of about four years old with a giant chocolate milk mustache on his upper lip. He is naked except for a pair of bright yellow swimming shorts. He takes one look at us and runs away, kicking up his skinny little boy knees, screaming, "Daddy! Students!"

I hear a frustrated "Oh!" and then footsteps from inside the living room.

Suddenly, we're face to face with him. We are looking at John Phillips.

He's a small man, smaller than Dad. He has a parrot nose, and a receding hair line. His eyes are brown and beady, and he has an overbite that makes his upper lip jut out. He's very skinny, and his hands are long-fingered and thin-looking. He's wearing very thick, heavy glasses that are sliding down his nose. Two red marks remain between his eyes, showing where his glasses are supposed to be. He's holding a lot of papers, and they're fanning from his hand, looking like they're about to slide out of his grasp.

He looks at us warily. "Can I help you?"

We stare at him. I glance at Xander, whose eyes have wandered down to his house slippers, which are two stuffed green frogs sitting on top of lily pad feet.

He is not at all how I imagined.

"If you're here to get into my Chaucer class, I'm sorry, but I'm already over-enrolled," he says, and gives us a distant, professional smile. "I'll offer it again next fall."

"We're Marie Vogel's daughters," Xander tells him.

"What?" Breathless.

The papers he's holding drop to the floor in a crashing flurry.

PHILLIPS

I'm glad he dropped his papers, because it gives us something to do. We help him pick them up. Xander even lies down on her stomach to get one that fell behind the couch. Finally he has them all stacked together. As I watch him line up the corners of the papers perfectly, I realize he's stalling. He is completely stunned, and he doesn't know what to do.

Finally he seems to understand that any more tidying of papers would be ludicrous, and he puts them down on the coffee table, which is strewn with Legos.

He straightens up, wiping his palms on the front of his plaid shirt, and stares at us.

Xander shifts her weight from one foot to the other. I clear my throat and immediately regret the sound. Desperately I search for a way to set everyone in motion again, but I have only one idea. Since no one else is talking, I say it out loud. "Could I have a glass of water?"

"Sure!" He sort of bounces on his toes, which makes me think he must be a jogger or something. People that old don't bounce unless they exercise. He leads us to the back of the house to a very messy kitchen. A box of cereal is on its side, spilled all over the white kitchen island. "Jeremy!" Phillips yells. "I told you I'd *help* you get the prize!" He scoops up a couple handfuls, but quickly gives up and gets a cup out of the dishwasher. He fills it with water from a jug on the counter and hands it to me. I take a small sip because I'm not entirely convinced that the cup is actually clean.

"So," he says shakily. "If you want the statue . . ."

"Oh, no! Keep it. You should have it," Xander says. "That's not why we're here."

His dark eyes dart between us warily, like he's expecting a coordinated attack. "Then why *are* you here?"

The hysterical way he asks the question shows how totally bewildered he is.

Xander looks at me and takes a step back, like she's giving me the stage.

Somehow I make my voice work. "We came here because we want to know. Did you and our mother—" I can't make myself say it.

"—do it?" Xander finishes.

"We're worried," I talk over her. "We're worried you had an affair."

He drops his chin to his chest. He hangs it there for a long time, his eyes screwed shut. When he finally opens his eyes, it's with total resignation. "Wait here."

He trots out of the room, and we hear him climbing some stairs. Xander reaches for my glass of water and takes a sip.

My heart is aching, throbbing, groaning in my chest.

Finally he comes down holding an envelope in his hand. He gestures toward a room off the kitchen, and we follow him into a small study with a ratty couch and a glossy wooden desk. This is probably where he comes to hide from his family when he works, just like Dad hides in the basement. He gestures for us to sit on the couch, and he takes the desk chair, resting the envelope on his knee, his fingers placed protectively over it.

"Before your mother died, she sent me the bird statue with this letter," he says authoritatively. Suddenly he's the professor again, which must be a shield he's putting up between us, like he has to remind himself we're no older than his students. "I'll let you read it first. And then I'll answer your questions as best I can."

He hands us the envelope. Xander takes it from him, unfolds it reverently, and holds it down on her lap so that we can both read it at the same time.

Dear John,

I hope this letter finds you well. I'm writing because I have some terrible news. I have breast cancer, and they've only given me another few months. When I found out I was sick, I wanted to call you. I should have. But I know you've remarried, and I want you to be happy. I suppose I still feel guilty about everything that happened, and so I've kept my distance.

The last time I saw you, I'm afraid I was cruel. I'm sorry for that.

Every time I look at those doves, it makes my heart hurt a little. I remember you so well, especially now that I have so much time to sit here and think. Please know that you were a great love in my life. Part of me wanted to come with you. But in the end, I had to make the choice I knew I could live with.

I could not believe a love that begins in the destruction of a family has a chance of surviving. This is how I learned to let you go. I taught myself to believe that we would not have been happy together. Despite my sadness over you, I have been very happy with James and the girls. If any family could mend a torn heart, it is mine.

But still know that I think of you often. In these last moments of my life, I've wished so much that we could say goodbye.

I'm a very lucky woman to have been loved by two men such as you and James. To know you both, to love you, has been a great honor.

I'm returning these doves to you, John, to enjoy and remember

*me by. I wish you a long life and tremendous happiness with your
family. Take it from one who knows, every moment you have with
them is precious.*
   Yours always,
   Marie

Xander finishes before I do, and she raises her eyes to John's. "So
you did? You did have an affair?"

"I'm afraid so."

The words drop like chunks of ice, making the room cold.

Phillips looks between the two of us, seeming to comprehend
something. "Oh, no!" He leans forward, his elbows on his knees.
"When we met, *I* was married. That's why she didn't want you girls
to know. She was ashamed she'd had an affair with a married man."

Xander wilts against me. I lean back against the couch. I never
thought of this. Never once. Slowly the stunned feeling seeps out
of me.

"I wish I could say something that would absolve her." He
stands up, walks behind his desk chair, and leans against the back of
it as he talks. His eyes remain on Mom's letter, which rests in Xander's lap. "We were very young. And I'd married a woman who
wasn't good for me. Who made me unhappy. But it was wrong."

"What about our dad?" Xander asks. I don't have to look at her
to know she's trying hard not to cry. "Was she already with Dad at
the time?"

"No." He slices the air with his hand as if trying to cut away any
doubt. "Not at first. She began dating him shortly before she and
I split."

The room is deadly quiet. Through the open door I hear a tele-
vision come on, some sticky-sweet children's program. The little boy
giggles. He's so lucky not to know about this.

"Look, girls," John says. "Your mother was a very good person
who made a mistake. She realized how serious it was before I did.

And she was the one who broke it off. Long before she married your father."

"But why did you send her the statue *after* she got married?" Xander asks. Her eyes are hard, and I realize that she doesn't trust what he's telling us.

He takes a deep breath. "Because my first wife left me after Marie married James. Your father. And I wanted Marie back."

"So you tried to steal her away from Dad?"

"I sent her the statue with a note that I was in town and would be waiting for her in a hotel room." The memory seems to sap his strength, and he sits down in the chair again.

"Did she come?"

He looks at us both, seeming to measure us. "Yes. She did. She tried to give me back the statue, but I wouldn't take it. And she left. I never saw her after that." He blinks twice, and I see a glisten in his eyes. Quickly he lifts his fingers to his face as though checking for tears.

"You really loved her," Xander says quietly.

For the first time, he smiles at us. "Of course I did."

Who She Loved More

Now I can almost see whatever it was Mom saw in him. He's small, and skinny, and his face is pleasant, not really handsome. But when he smiles, his face takes on a masculine quality that reminds me of Adam somehow. There's something very decent about him.

I look at Xander. Her expression is still hard. She doesn't believe him.

The phone rings somewhere in the back of the house, and I hear little feet running for it, then a squeaky "Hello?" followed by "Daddy!"

"Just a moment," John says to us before getting up.

Once he's out of the room, Xander darts off the couch. "Are you buying this?"

"Yes." I'm sick of her suspicions. "He's given us no reason to doubt him. You saw Mom's letter."

She half shrugs, then plops back down on the couch, arms crossed over her middle.

I hear the murmur of John's voice. By the tone I'd judge he's not talking to a student. There's none of the professional distance in his voice, but there is a nervousness, as though he's a little afraid of the person he's talking to. Slowly his voice gets louder as he makes his way back to the study, and his words become clear. "They seem fine to me . . ."

I look at Xander. She is staring at me with round eyes.

"They're right here . . . I'll get them . . ." John comes back in the room and holds out the phone to Xander. Of course she waves it away, the coward, so he hands it to me and stands by the window.

"H-hi, Dad," I stammer.

"Do you have *any idea* what you've put me through?" He is literally snarling.

"I'm sorry!"

"Answer my question!"

"I thought it was rhetorical."

"Are you seriously going to give me attitude at a time like this?" This is just like something Mom would say. To hear it come from Dad sounds a little weird, but somehow comforting too. "You are grounded for the rest of the summer."

"We probably deserve it."

Xander is biting her bottom lip as she listens. She has broken into a sweat.

"How did you find us?" I ask.

"Nancy told me you've been sniffing around the whole John Phillips thing. Asking questions, reading your mother's documents, snooping around, and generally being two hideous little miscreants." I have never known my dad to be so angry. I can actually hear his spit hitting the phone as he talks. "Who told you to go around asking questions? Your mother's past is *none* of your business!"

"Nancy wasn't supposed to say anything! We didn't want this to hurt you!"

"Nancy didn't tell me anything I didn't already know. "

This stops me cold. All this time we could have asked Dad about this. We could have avoided so much heartache! "So you know about Mom and John Phillips?"

"Of course I do. She was gone for two days—you think I wouldn't notice that?" He clips the last word, as though trying to bite back the whole sentence.

Two days.

"She was gone for *two days?*" I ask him, my eyes on Phillips. His face colors.

Xander's head pops up.

The line is silent for a couple beats. "What did he tell you?"

I can hardly make my voice work. It feels like rusty gears. "That she went to see him at his hotel and left right away."

Phillips drops his head into his hands and hides there. Xander stands up and paces back and forth behind the coffee table, two steps up, two steps back, like a caged cougar.

The phone line is quiet for so long that I begin to wonder if Dad hung up, but then he clears his throat. His voice is thready. "Nancy is booking me on the next plane out there. I'll be there at eight o'clock this evening. You're to drive to the airport to meet me."

"Dad!" I say, trying to cling to him somehow with my voice. I feel like the whole fabric of my life has been shredded and all I have are tendrils of false memory.

"We'll talk about this later," he says, and hangs up.

I put the phone down on the coffee table in front of my knees. Phillips sinks into his desk chair again. Xander and I both stand over him, waiting for an explanation. He does not meet our eyes, just rubs at his Adam's apple, seeming to think through some complicated problem in his head.

Xander sits back down. In a deep, threatening voice, she says, "Start again. The truth this time."

He spins his chair a half turn and looks out the window behind his desk. I look too. There's a hummingbird feeder outside, and a tiny little buzzing bird darts around it, sucking at sugar water with its long, thin beak.

I turn to see Phillips working his mouth like he's trying to relearn how to form words. "She didn't want you to know," he said. "That's why I lied."

"I need the *truth*." Xander is crying. I don't have to look at her face to know that.

I'm not crying. I'm too numb.

He looks at the floor as he speaks, each word carefully considered before it is laid before us. "She came to my hotel room. She was crying, and holding the bird statue. She wanted to give it back to me. She said she had a new life now and she needed to forget about me."

I have to look at the floor. I can't look at his strained face as he talks.

"I wouldn't take it. And I asked . . . begged her to just stay with me. Just to talk. She'd had an argument with James, and every time she tried to leave, I took advantage of her confused feelings and I got her to stay." The room is silent for a while, and I hear the weird, distant sound of a children's song coming from the TV. The strangeness of the contrast between this room and that room turns my stomach.

"I thought when Marie left Hanover to be with your dad that I could somehow put the pieces of my own life back together. I tried to make it work with my first wife. I really did, but something had died between us, and she finally gave up. She knew that I was still in love with your mother."

Something in his voice changes, and I look at him. With a jolt, I see that his eyes are on me, and there's such longing and sadness in his expression, I realize that he's seeing Mom in me. I pick up a couch pillow and bury my face in it. I can't have him looking at me that way. It just makes me know all over again that Mom is dead and Xander and I are all that's left of her.

"By then, your mother was married, but I came for her anyway. It took a lot of talking, and coaxing, but I got her to listen to me. And for about twenty-four hours, I had her convinced that she and I belonged together." I hear a strange sound and look up to see that he's chuckling to himself, though there's no humor in it. "That was the happiest twenty-four hours of my life. Until Jeremy was born, that is."

The room feels stuffy, like the air is too thick to breathe or talk through. My mind is jammed up, and I can't make myself think. When someone finally speaks, it's Xander. "Where were we during all this?"

He smiles sadly. "With your grandmother. You don't remember any of this?"

We both shake our heads. "We'd have been toddlers still," Xander says.

We're all awkward, and silent, until Xander speaks. "In her note, Mom said she was sorry for being cruel." It's not a question, but she's asking something.

He rubs his scalp with his fingertips, back and forth, hard. "We spent the night in my hotel, and the next day we decided that the best thing would be to leave town, let your dad get used to the idea. She always planned on coming to get you girls when the dust settled. I want to make that absolutely clear. She contemplated leaving your father, but never you. Never."

His gaze is steady as he pauses, looking at both of us, willing us to believe him. And I do. I know he's not lying. At least this much I know about Mom. She would never have abandoned me and Xander. She loved us too much. It doesn't really help, though, knowing that she wanted to take us from our dad. It feels sickening to know how close my family came to breaking apart forever.

"But she came back," Xander says, her voice sounding dry like frayed cotton.

"We got as far as Montpelier before she *made* me turn back."

He stops there, but Xander and I only wait. The story isn't finished. I need to know everything.

He sighs. "I tried to convince her. I begged her. She had to scream at me because I refused to understand. She finally said, 'I love James more than you.'" He tries to laugh, but his eyes are sad. "'I love him more.' That's how she was cruel, since you want to know."

He shakes his head; his gaze drops. By his expression, which is full of pain, I know for sure. This is exactly what Mom said to him.
I love James more.

The room is quiet, except for the faint sound of cartoons. Finally Xander speaks. "Can we see it?"

He is boneless in his chair, his eyes rubbed raw, his skin sallow. He looks like someone who has just gotten over a terrible disease. He nods, and leads us through his house, to the back behind the kitchen. It's a tiny pantry, barely large enough for the three of us to stand in, filled with soup cans and boxes dusted with flour. John reaches to the top shelf and pulls down a small shipping box that is hanging open with lots of bubble wrap spilling out. He holds it, staring into the box for what seems like a long time. Then he swallows, audibly, and hands the box to Xander.

"Actually, girls, I would like you to take it."

"No," I say. My voice sounds very loud in this tiny room. "Mom wanted you to have it."

"It meant enough that she remembered me at the end." He pushes the box into Xander's stomach and closes her hands around it, folding her fingers gently around the corners of the cardboard. "I mean it. I've got a family now. And a wonderful wife. I shouldn't let my house get crowded up with ghosts."

I want to tell him no again, but Xander nods. "I understand that," she says.

He leads us to the front door and opens it for us. John's little boy turns around when he sees us and yells, "Swimming, Daddy!"

"Five minutes," John tells him. He turns to look at me and Xander, his sad eyes darting between us. "You both look so much like—"

"Thanks," Xander interrupts. It's too painful to let him finish.

He nods in understanding. "Thank you for coming to see me."

"Goodbye," Xander says, and turns to go to the car.

Something pulls me, or pushes, and though I don't want to do it, I step forward and kiss John on the cheek. His stubble tickles my bottom lip, and a spark of electricity snaps from my fingers to his shoulder. If I hadn't stopped believing Mom was still in the world, I would imagine that spark is a message for him from her. When I pull away, his face is rubbery and undone. I can't make myself speak, so I run to the car.

We drive off without looking back.

We've gotten what we wanted. We have the answers. And considering what it might have been, the story came to a conclusion that I can live with. Mom didn't cheat on us for years. She slipped up for a couple days. So why don't I feel better?

I look at Xander in the rearview mirror. She's squinting through the bright windshield at the street, looking sullen and angry. She doesn't feel any better either.

Adam knows enough not to ask us about it right away. He just drives, waiting patiently for us to tell him when we're ready. But what will we say?

That Mom didn't have an affair so much as a couple days of temptation. That she came to her senses and ran back to Dad, who forgave her. It doesn't really matter, in the end, how many men Mom loved, because it turns out we don't feel any better. We solved the mystery, got the answers we were looking for, and now we're back where we started.

Mom is dead. John Phillips was just one facet of her life that we didn't know about. But there were a million facets to the diamond that was Marie Vogel, and the only ones we ever got to see were of her being our mom. The mischievous teenager, the brilliant academic mind, the confused lover, the torn heart, all of these were parts of her too, but we never knew these sides of her, and we never will. No matter how many mysteries we solve, no matter how many road trips we go on looking for the key to Mom's past, she's never coming back. Except for the letters she wrote to us, there's no way we can ever know more about her than we already do. Mom's life is a closed book we can never read.

It's like we were trying to build a bridge to wherever Mom is. But that's impossible. Not only did we lose Marie the mother, we lost all of her, and we lost the chance to know the rest of her. Forever.

I've been talking to her in my mind since she died, trying to convince myself it wasn't true. But it is. Mom is gone.

I let out a little groan and lie down on the seat, shielding my eyes with my arm. I hear Xander's breath come in starts and hiccups, and I know she's buried her face in Adam's shirt and she's quietly crying, just like I am.

Dinner in a Tacky Hotel

Dad looks like he's aged about twenty years when he comes through the airport gate. His eyes are baggy, and his hair hangs in his eyes. He walks bent over, looking at the floor, so that he almost bumps into us before he notices we're standing right in front of him. Xander and I smile sheepishly, but he doesn't return our smiles. He seems brokenhearted, and I feel even worse about making him worry so much. Adam takes his garment bag from him and we lead him out to the parking garage. He walks to the driver's side and snaps his fingers. Adam gives him the car keys without a word.

We're on the highway, on the way to the hotel Nancy booked for us, before Dad finally says a direct word to Xander and me. "I really don't know what to say to you."

"Daddy, I'm sorry," Xander pleads. She's in the front seat next to him, and she leans forward, trying to get him to look at her, but he won't. "We tried to get permission. We really did."

"And I said *no!*" Dad punches the steering wheel. The car swerves, and the driver next to us honks his horn. Dad tries to calm himself down with deep, shaky breaths. "I lost my wife, not even a year ago! For twenty-four hours you made me think I might have lost the two of you as well. Do you know what that did to me? Do you?"

Xander shrinks back into her seat. She almost never has this look on her face, but it's written all over her profile. She's totally ashamed.

"Adam, your mother has been through enough without you wandering off."

"I know," he says. He's staring at the back of Xander's head with worry.

We all brood as Dad pulls in to the hotel parking lot, and we pile out and go check in to our rooms, Adam and Dad in one, Xander and me in the other. It's a nice room, decorated with burgundy and gold curtains and plush, squishy carpeting. It's almost nine o'clock, and I'd love to ignore my empty belly and crawl between the sheets, but Dad knocks on our door and calls, "Let's go have some dinner."

Xander and I follow him down the hallway. The carpeting is so thick, I can't hear our footsteps. Dad seems a little less furious now, but he still seems heartbroken. I'm starving, but I'm so filled with dread about what he's going to say to us, I can't imagine eating a big heavy meal. What I really want is Cream of Wheat, the way Mom used to make it when we were little. She would drop cut-up dried apples and apricots into it, and drizzle honey on top. I've tried making it for myself, but I can never make it taste the way Mom could. That's one more thing I wish I'd asked her. How did you make that Cream of Wheat?

"Vanilla," she whispers in the sound of the elevator doors opening for us.

Of course. Vanilla.

But that wasn't Mom. It was my subconscious or something. Wishful thinking. And I've got to let that go. I can't keep hurting like this, and talking to a figment of my imagination isn't helping me.

"Where's Adam?" Xander asks worriedly.

"He's getting room service," Dad says. "He thought we'd want to be alone to talk."

Xander rolls her eyes. I know just how she feels. I sometimes wish Adam weren't so damn appropriate all the time. Now Dad can really let us have it without worrying about appearances.

We are seated at a comfortable corner booth, and we can hear the fountain that's in the middle of the room, drizzling water over mossy, jagged rocks. The waiter is very soft-spoken and polite, and he takes our drink orders right away. Mint tea for me, Diet Coke for Xander, and a martini on the rocks for Dad, which shows how upset he is. He hardly ever drinks hard liquor.

He weaves his fingers together and looks at us. We stare at one another long enough for the waiter to bring our drinks and take our orders. When he leaves, Dad takes a sip, and another, sets his glass down, and finally speaks. "Why didn't you come to me about Phillips?"

I look at Xander, who is staring into her lap as though she's making a breakthrough about the construction of blue jeans. So I say, "We were afraid that Mom had an affair with him, and if that was true, we didn't want you to know."

His eyes are electrified with rage, and his voice seems to crackle. "You imagined that you knew something about my relationship with your mother that I didn't?"

"We wanted to protect you," Xander says quietly. "You've been a little . . . fragile lately."

"This is how you protect me? By disappearing for two days . . ." He breaks off, his tired eyes wandering over the table.

Two days. Xander and I look at each other, and I can tell she's realizing the same thing I am—that our leaving reminded him of how Mom left with Phillips all those years ago. And when he finally found us, who had we gone to see?

How could we have been so selfish?

"I'm so sorry, Dad," I whisper.

"Me too," Xander says.

"We just thought—"

"What?" he spits angrily. "That your mother was a cheater?"

"We could never have imagined that there was another man in Mom's life, and when we found out there was . . ." Xander trails off.

I can't stop a tear from falling down my face. "I felt like I didn't know her all of a sudden."

Dad glares at us both, but when he sees the pain on our faces, his anger seems to melt away a little, and he lets out a long, low sigh. "Girls, your mother was exactly who you thought she was. She never misrepresented herself to anyone. She was always honest with me about her feelings for John, and when those feelings faded away, she was honest about that too."

I lift my eyes to Dad's. He's still angry, but at least now he's trying to do something. He's trying to be our dad, maybe for the first time in almost a year.

Xander must see it too, because she says, "I missed you, Dad."

This does something to him, and he leans back in his chair as though he's suddenly too tired to sit up straight. For a second I have the insane idea that Xander has ruined it and with a few short words Dad has gone back to being the same boneless heap he's been for the past year.

The way we're all sitting here, dazed and sad, reminds me of how we all looked the night after Mom's funeral, when everyone had left and we were all alone, the three of us, newly aware that one of us was missing, and would be forever. Xander was pale and wan, Dad looked gray and angry. My eyes looked huge and shocked, as though the rest of my skull had shrunk from sadness. I remember I felt that something in the world had gone terribly, terribly wrong, and that we had lost our chance forever to fix it.

Soon the waiter brings our orders, which surprises me because I don't really remember ordering. BLT for Xander, French dip for me, grilled cod for Dad. I eat mechanically. I can hear Xander chewing and swallowing, and I want to tell her to stop being such a pig. But I hold my tongue. At least everyone is eating, proof that this isn't really so bad as the night after Mom's funeral. Nothing could be that bad.

"Look, girls, I know deep in my heart that your mother loved me totally, and I her." His eyes flash with the passion of what he's saying. "We loved each other more every day. I have absolutely no doubt about that. Okay?" he says sternly.

"Okay," we both whisper.

Dad pushes his plate away. He leans his elbows on the table and looks at Xander with a steady eye, and then at me. "I'm sorry, girls."

Xander looks up from her half-eaten dill pickle. I put down my sandwich, which is clammy and cold.

"I've been so sad." He rubs his whole face with one big hand. "I haven't really been there for you."

"That's okay," Xander tells him. She reaches across the table and rubs his shoulder. "We understood."

"You needed me," he insists. "I shouldn't have left you girls alone to figure out what to do with all your grief."

"Is there any other way?" I ask.

He crinkles his eyebrows, not understanding.

I remember the portraits Aunt Doris painted of Mom, and it helps me formulate the idea into words. "I think everyone does their grieving alone."

Dad's face softens. In spite of what I've done to him over the past forty-eight hours, he seems proud of me. "You might be right about that."

Xander makes a face. "How come she always gets to be the wise one?"

Dad smiles a real smile. "Because it's your job to be the smart-ass."

We all laugh, weakly. Dad doesn't seem furious anymore.

The waiter comes to take our plates away and asks if we want dessert. Xander nods emphatically, and soon we're eating enormous hot fudge sundaes, extra nuts for me and Dad, extra whipped cream for Xander. She has a dot of white on the end of her nose because she always takes too big of bites, but Dad and I don't tell her. We smirk at each other as she prattles on about how she can hardly wait to get some lab time at Caltech, she just hopes they let freshmen use the electron microscope or the particle splitter or laser doohickey. Something like that—I'm not really listening.

After we finish our ice cream, we all lean back. Xander rubs her belly unabashedly. Dad burps kind of loudly, then whispers, "Excuse me," his face red.

We feel like a family again. One of us is missing, but somehow we closed the circle.

What is it about ice cream that can do that?

"So, Dad, who's sending our letters?" Xander asks. She leans forward, testing her boundaries, as always.

I elbow her in the ribs. She can never let go of anything.

He looks at her, his eyes narrowed, and he clips his words as he answers. "Your grandmother. Which you probably could have found out had you visited her on Mother's Day as your mother asked you to do."

This shuts Xander up for a good long time.

THE LAST DAY

IT'S SO EARLY, the robins aren't singing yet. I can hear a warbler in the oak tree by Adam's house. One by one, more birds answer his call.

Xander and I are standing on the front porch with her mountain of luggage between us. Most of the clothes in her bags are new from a shopping spree we went on last week. The shirts she bought have a plunging neckline, and the pants are snug around the hips, but it's a vast improvement over the ripped jeans and halter tops she's been wearing lately. "I'm de-skanking for college," she announced to one saleslady at Macy's, who kept her distance after that.

Dad bought her a new laptop with enough memory to handle the kind of data she'll be crunching in her research projects at Caltech. Nancy got her a fax machine/printer, and Adam bought her a gold necklace with a heart-shaped pendant. He engraved something on the back, initials that stand for a private joke between them. Xander won't tell me what it means, but that's okay. I don't need to know.

"You'll e-mail me, right?" Xander asks me, biting her lip. She doesn't usually let herself look scared, but today she's not hiding anything.

"Of course I'll e-mail you. You better answer."

"I will."

"None of this, 'I read it and couldn't respond right away, and then I forgot' crap. Answer me *right away*."

"I will! God!" she says, but she has a sad smile on her face. She looks over at Adam's house. The downstairs lights have come on, and we catch glimpses of Adam and Nancy rushing around, getting things ready. Nancy won't take him to the airport for another two hours, but they got up early to come say goodbye to Xander before she leaves this morning.

It's probably best that they're leaving on the same day. It will be easier than watching one of them go, and then the other. To be really honest about it, I'd say that what I'm feeling isn't so much sadness as fear. I've never known a life without Xander stirring things up and Adam calming things down. I'm not sure I even know what *I'll* be like without them. Without Xander as my counterbalance, will I still be Zen? Or will I be plain old Athena Vogel, with nothing and no one to define me?

Finally Adam and Nancy come out with his black luggage— two large duffel bags and an overstuffed garment bag. Once they have everything stacked and ready, they stop puttering around and just stare at us from across the street. Xander holds up her hand.

"Aren't you guys a little early?" Xander asks as Adam saunters across the street, one hand in the front pocket of his jeans.

"So?" is his answer.

He stands at the edge of our lawn and looks up at Xander like he's Romeo and she's Juliet. For a while it seemed like they would kill each other like Shakespeare's lovers, but now it looks like they finally accepted they can't live without each other. They're both much nicer people now that they finally gave in to it.

"You're looking very collegey," Nancy tells her as she bounds up the porch steps.

She means the beautiful wool blazer Mom ordered for Xander, which was delivered yesterday by Grandma in a large pink box. Its gray-brown color brings out Xander's eyes. When she tried it on, she had to blink back tears. "It's beautiful," she whispered to Grandma, who only nodded, looking very proud that she was the one who could bring it to her. There was a note from Mom, too, that said, *I'm more proud of you than I can say.*

I got a note too:

> *Dear Zen,*
>
> *It must be so hard to be left behind, first by me, and now by Xander. I wish there was something I could say to ease your heart right now, but I think you'll just have to feel the pain.*
>
> *Xander isn't just your sister. You know that, don't you? Not all sisters have what you have. Don't let go of it. There is a precious silver thread you can always walk across to find each other, wherever you are, in whatever holes you've dug for yourselves. I feel better about leaving knowing you have each other. You always will.*
>
> *You're going to find your own way. You're going to become the woman you were always meant to be.*
>
> *Love always,*
> *Mom*

It was the perfect letter for today, for saying goodbye.

Because Mom's not here to do it, Nancy engulfs Xander in a big hug. "God, I'm going to miss the trouble you cause," she says.

"Well," Xander says casually, "keep your eye on the news. You never know."

"You make headlines, kid, I'll disown you," Nancy says. She wipes her eyes with her shirtsleeve and heads inside. "I hope your father is making coffee."

"He's trying," I tell her.

I take a seat on the porch swing and look off toward the sunrise, which is just starting to pink up the sky. "Cheer up," Mom whispers in the call of a chickadee twittering in a lilac bush. "Cheer up up up."

But it's not her. It's a bird.

From the corner of my eye I watch Xander and Adam hanging on to each other, swaying back and forth. They stay like that for a long time, just holding each other quietly, like they're hoping they might get stuck that way and they won't have to say goodbye. I hear a soft little sob from Xander, and so I get up and go inside to find Nancy, Dad, and some coffee.

When we come back out with a big tray of reheated cinnamon rolls, a pot of strong coffee, and five mugs, they're still holding each other right where I left them. Nancy clears her throat, and they finally pull apart, reluctantly, like strips of Velcro.

Dad pours a cup for everyone, and we all sit back down, Xander and Adam on the steps, me and Nancy on the porch swing, and Dad on the bench by the door. I imagine Mom hovering near the spider web that's tangled in the railing, glistening with dew. Mom always found spider webs fascinating, and she'd stare at them, following the course of the thin silk threads, trying to see how the spider wove it. She'd say, "Don't tell me that isn't a form of intelligence. *Look* at it!"

It's a good web, and if she were alive today, that's where she'd be standing, looking at it to distract herself from the fact that Xander is leaving home forever.

Suddenly the feeling of Mom being with us on the porch is so strong, I can almost trick my eyes into seeing her there, her dark eyes trailing through the web as the first morning sunlight plays in its strands.

She turns toward me and smiles.

"Do you guys ever feel like Mom's here with us?" I ask before I even know the words are in my mind.

My question goes unanswered, because Dad is completely unraveled by it. He hides his face in his hand and whispers, "She should be here to see you off."

Nancy leans forward and gives his back a little pat.

I look at Xander, who is watching me, a strange expression on her face. Her eyes dart over to the spider web and hang there for a second, almost as if she sees Mom there too, before darting back to me again. She blinks slowly, a faint smile on her lips.

I love my sister.

When there's no more time to linger, we all stand up, and Dad parks the Audi in front. Everyone grabs a bag and we load up the car, and Dad walks around to get into the driver's seat. Dad's driving Xander to the airport alone because she doesn't want a big goodbye scene in public. Adam, Nancy, and I all stand around awkwardly, waiting to see what she'll do.

Xander chooses Nancy first, grabbing both sides of her face with her hands and squeezing her cheeks. An odd thing to do, but since Nancy is odd, she seems to understand completely what this means. "I love you to pieces," she tells Xander through her squished-together cheeks.

Xander laughs because it looks so funny. "I love you too."

Xander releases her, and Nancy turns away because she's crying. She waves without turning around and jogs into her house.

Now it's just Adam and me, looking at her. I take half a step forward because I'm sure her last goodbye, the place of honor, will be for him, but she surprises me, and turns to him with a radiant smile.

He steps forward and takes hold of her hand.

"Everything to me" is all she can say.

He nods, but he can't speak. He grabs on to her and holds her, staring off angrily at Lake Champlain, which is starting to glow brilliantly with the rising sun.

They don't say anything. He lets go of her abruptly, and he runs off, pounding up the porch stairs and into his house just like Nancy did.

She gives me a wry smile through her tears. "He'll never get over me."

"Over you?"

She shrugs. "I mean, Jesus, Zen. I'm eighteen years old. What am I going to do? *Marry* him?"

"I thought—"

"The future will come how it comes." She says this bravely, with some resignation. With the palm of her hand, she scrubs her face free of tears. "Do I look okay?" she asks.

"You look like my sister," I tell her.

She turns away, toward Lake Champlain, just the way Adam did. "You will always be, until the day I die, my best friend in the whole world."

I look again at the lilac bush. The chickadee is still there, hopping from branch to branch. I can't look at Xander as I speak, but somehow that feels right. "Me too."

We don't hug. The Vogel sisters don't hug. She touches the tips of her fingers to my forehead, gives me an aching smile, and turns to get in the car.

Once inside, she rolls down the window and gives me her brattiest sneer. "Oh, by the way, I gave the lovebirds to Adam."

A shriek of anger bolts through my throat. "Why didn't you *ask?*"

"You would have said no."

Her voice is defiant, but her eyes are full of deep sorrow. My anger fades, because I know what it means to her, to give Mom's statue to him.

"Well, as long as there's a good chance it'll stay in the family."

"A chance," she murmurs, wistful, as she rolls up the window.

She places her palm on the glass. I place my palm there too.

We stay like that, looking at each other, until Dad revs the engine.

I watch them drive away until the car gets lost in the glare on the lake.

The house feels empty. I wonder if Mom is sitting next to Xander on the plane, making sure she gets there okay. I don't know if I'm kidding myself about that or not. I'll never know. But I suppose I can believe what makes me feel better. That's probably what Paul would say. I've just said goodbye to Adam before he and Nancy drove off, and now I'm on the porch swing, trying to read a book.

There's a pit in my stomach a mile deep.

I keep catching my eye on the same sentence over and over again, but it won't sink in. I want them all back, but I can't go back. I'm stuck on this swing, moving around but staying in the same place.

I hear gravel skipping, and I look down the street to see Paul walking along, his camera around his neck, his hands in his pockets. When he sees me, he smiles, and I notice for the first time that his teeth are a little off center from the rest of his face, which gives him the grin of a scoundrel. I like it.

"Whatcha doing?" he asks me.

"Everyone left today," I say tearfully.

His posture droops, and he sits down next to me on the porch swing and gives me a long-faced look of commiseration. "You okay?" He rests his hand on my foot, pats it a few times. I like how he touches me. We communicate so easily that way.

"I'm okay."

He gives me a sly, sideways look, and asks with a grin, "Know what time it is?"

I peek through the living room curtains at the mantel clock. "It's almost noon."

I realize what he's getting at, and I have to smile.

"We have time to catch it if we hurry." He stands up and holds out his hand.

I take it, and the pit in my stomach sinks away.

We jog most of the way, and we make it to the bridge just in time.

It had coal, lots of huge logs, and stacks of bright shiny cars.

And the engineer got an eyeful too.

My thanks to Margaret Raymo
and the team at Houghton Mifflin Harcourt
for their support and excellence,
and to Kathleen Anderson, for her wisdom.
And as always, my loving thanks to
Richard, who reads, listens,
and loves.